"At a time when many young gay writers are forgetting their queer lineage, Philip Dean Walker comes along and schools us with his debut short story collection. Here is Halston, Liza, and Warhol at Studio 54; here is a drag queen who rivals Josephine Baker's star appeal; and here is, in Walker's words, the boy who lived next to the boys next door, dead during the early plague years, but resurrected through Walker's alluring prose, prose that renders the past our present. These stories are clever and do not apologize for their cleverness, like Rock Hudson, who explains here, 'Handsome men know they're handsome. There was no reason to be coy or overly modest about it—that kind of thing just reeked of phoniness to him.' Phony, these stories are not. From the Castro to Grey Gardens, I travelled gleefully alongside Walker in *At Danceteria and Other Stories*, and am only disappointed the journey had to end."

—D. Gilson, author of
I Will Say This Exactly One Time: Essays

"Reading Philip Dean Walker is like being swept into the defiantly glittering rooms of tragedy-darkened souls. Walker's *At Danceteria and Other Stories* testifies to the tart-tongued power of language to resurrect and witness, in tales that are screamingly funny and hauntingly sad. His men and women radiate an alluring self-awareness and fallibility that touches our deepest places."

—Elise Levine, author of *Driving Men Mad*

"This highly original meditation on the '80s is like nothing else you've read. Dead celebrities are brought back to life in the oddest places: Jackie O in a New York sex club, Princess Di in a London drag bar, Rock Hudson at the White House. Plus Sylvester, Halston and Liza, Keith Haring, Madonna, and, best of all, an anonymous narrator who notices that only good-looking guys in New York are getting the new gay cancer. Odd conjunctions, great wit, and the shadow of AIDS make these stories deceptively light and strangely disturbing."

—Andrew Holleran, author of *Dancer from the Dance*

"In his debut collection, *At Danceteria and Other Stories*, Philip Dean Walker writes with a kind of savage nostalgia, one that knows the past was not prettier or glitzier or more fabulous—only more terrifying. Set in the early 1980s, when the word 'queer' was still an insult and when doctors and nurses invented their own names for the mysterious disease killing beautiful young men, *At Danceteria and Other Stories* brutally exposes how what we don't know about ourselves can kill us. Walker's writing is vivid, electric, and devastating."

—Stephanie Grant, author of *The Passion of Alice*

"These stories—so funny and inventive, so merciless, smart, and affecting—are like no others I know, populated with American celebutantes, like Liza Minnelli, Jackie Kennedy, and Little Edie Beale, and punctuated by an abiding American loneliness that has the power to break one's heart. Walker's stories are fully, fully alive."

—Richard McCann, author of *Mother of Sorrows*

AT DANCETERIA
and other stories

Philip Dean Walker

SQUARES & REBELS
Minneapolis, MN

ACKNOWLEDGMENTS

The following stories have previously appeared in *Jonathan: A Queer Fiction Journal*:

"At Danceteria"
"The Boy Who Lived Next to the Boy Next Door"
"Charlie Movie Star"
"Don't Stop Me Now"

DISCLAIMER

This is a work of fiction. Names, characters, businesses, places, events, and incidents are either the products of the author's imagination or used in a fictitious manner. Even though celebrities and historical figures may be used as characters in these stories, their actions or dialogue should not be construed as factual or historical truths.

COPYRIGHT

To the memory of

Ruth Ellen Manchester (1925-2001)
and
Stewart Irving Buckley, Jr. (1953-1991)

"Only connect! That was the whole of her sermon. Only connect the prose and the passion, and both will be exalted, and human love will be seen at its height. Live in fragments no longer. Only connect, and the beast and the monk, robbed of the isolation that is life to either, will die."

—E. M. Forster, *Howards End* (1910)

By Halston
1

Don't Stop Me Now
19

Charlie Movie Star
30

The Boy Who Lived Next to the Boy Next Door
45

Sequins at Midnight
59

Jackie and Jerry and The Anvil
67

At Danceteria
87

By Halston

Liza is late to 101 East 63rd Street. Fashionably late, Halston thinks. Liza is always fashionably late to 101, but Halston doesn't care because he is often late too. After all, people *should* wait for him. They should always be waiting for him. Anticipation. It keeps people talking about you. He will routinely call for a meeting at 10 a.m. at Olympic Tower and then purposely show up an hour late. What are they going to do? Have the meeting without him? Hardly.

He should design a new fragrance and call it Anticipation. His first fragrance, simply called Halston, was the most successful designer fragrance of the last decade. He did it with Max Factor, and it really was a phenomenal success. Because *he* is a phenomenal success. So many triumphs, it's almost embarrassing to list them all. And tonight, he is convinced, will be no exception.

He snorts another line of cocaine off a rectangular mirror while wearing his mirrored sunglasses.

"So, where is the Queen of Broadway?" Steve yells from the top of 101's floating staircase.

Halston doesn't answer because, all of a sudden, Steve has reminded him of someone he hates. He reminds him of a faggy JCPenney button specialist (or whatever the person's title is—Halston can't be bothered with learning it) with whom he is now forced to work at his private offices in Olympic Tower. JCPenney, which is selling a new stylish (yet affordable) line of his fashions called Halston III, has a person who deals exclusively with the buttons.

His regular ready-to-wear line never uses buttons. They are seamless creations: no buttons, zippers, or unnecessary closures. Maybe one small hook-and-eye. They are sculpted to the body. They become part of the body. Skins of hammered silk, shirred matte jersey, and cashmere. Just the sound of a zipper makes him think of back-to-school sales, parking lots with weeds growing through cracks in the asphalt, and abused women covering up bruises with peach makeup in station wagons before entering department stores in Des Moines.

He doesn't want to ever have to answer Steve's question about Liza's whereabouts. And, he likely won't have to because Steve will forget he asked anyway. Halston waits for the inevitable moment in which Steve will proceed to shut the fuck up and bring him a Scotch.

As he bends down to do another line, Liza appears before him like a magic trick. Like she is Glinda the Good Witch in that big pink bubble in *The Wizard of Oz* with Liza's mother in the blue gingham dress. Liza. His Liza. He never even heard her open the door.

"Halston, darling. My driver is sick so I had to take a cab," Liza says, exasperated.

She is running her hands through her hair. It's pixie short again like she wore it when she got her first Oscar nomination for *The Sterile Cuckoo*. Or *Tell Me That You Love Me, Junie Moon*. He can't remember right now which came first. "You look fabulous, Halston. Just fabulous. They're going to love you tonight. It's just going to happen that way, I know it," she says, whipping off a black cashmere cape he designed for her to reveal the gold metallic jersey gown he also designed for her. He altered the design slightly in order to distinguish it from the gown that became part of the Halston Originals ready-to-wear line. He doesn't just design clothes for Liza. He designs Liza for her life.

"You look fabulous, too, babe. Faaaaabulous," he says.

"Oh, do you like this little number? It's by … Halston." She winks at him. The thick crème Bakelite bracelets she wears make a muted clank as she shakes with laughter. That Sally Bowles laugh he loves.

"Oh, well, then I adore it. But you're late. Here, kisses." He arches his back to extend his face to catch her kiss on his cheek as she makes her way to the sofa across from him. "Here, do this. Now." He motions toward the long line of coke he's set out on the mirror that he pushes across the table. The table is low to the floor and made out of glass. Several white orchids in gray ceramic vases are on the table alongside an oblong silver Elsa Perretti ashtray in the center. It's already halfway filled with cigarette butts. Halston smokes so many cigarettes on a typical evening that he has begun to see them as his actual fingers, each one lopped off his body after he has exhausted use of it. They're like part of a very chic exoskeleton that must be sloughed off at the end of each night so he can be reborn again anew in the morning.

Liza snorts up the line and then licks a finger to collect the leftover residue, wiping it onto her gums. Halston reaches over and does the same, but more delicately. With more flair. More panache. He does even the smallest things better than other people. Even the way he does drugs is artful. Liza licks another finger and imitates him, smiling.

"Hello, Steve!" Liza yells in the direction of upstairs. Steve appears at the balcony standing next to the silkscreen paintings hanging on the wall that Andy did of Halston and Liza. There are two images of Halston in different colors and one of Liza beneath him. Halston liked his so much that he used the image in an ad in 1974.

"Heya, Angel. I brought over two things to wear, and I was up here trying them both on," Steve says.

"Just put on the tux, Steve. Andy's meeting us there so we have to go. The limo is waiting," Halston says as he puts on a black jacket over a black ribbed turtleneck with Ultrasuede patches at the elbows. He throws on a white silk scarf that is hanging off the edge of a gray lacquered side table. Ultrasuede is ultracool. He brought the material out of nowhere and totally made it a thing. All of his sofas are made out of it. The men he invites over at night sit on Ultrasuede love seats, naked and full of admiration for him. Ultrasuede is ultracool.

"Fashion!" Liza says, her open palms framing her face, like she's peeking out of a closed curtain one last time at the end of a show.

They meet Andy in the main lobby of the American Museum of Natural History's Hall of Ocean Life where a party and a runway show to celebrate Halston III is taking place with over a thousand attendees. A red banner hanging across the entrance of the museum announces in white letters, "Introducing Halston III." Andy is wearing black sunglasses and a black jacket with a black shirt and a pink neon tie.

"That tie is very strange, Andy. I don't think I like it," says Halston.

"You didn't design it so you have to criticize it. I understand. Welcome to your party, Halston." Andy looks over his shoulder for a moment as if he is being followed or watched. "I don't like this museum. I never have. The cave people in the other wing feel threatening to me when I walk by them. I imagine them killing me when my back is turned, eating me, and then grunting together about how bad I taste."

"You don't like this museum because none of your paintings are in it," Halston says.

"Of course, well, there's that too," Andy says.

"I need a drink," Liza says. "Halston, are you nervous?"

He should be nervous. But somehow he isn't. He knows the line is good. And Liza knows he wouldn't even be here if he didn't think the line was good. But Halston III is not really something he's ever done before—it's affordable casual-wear. He has never sent a pair of jeans down a runway before, that's for sure. He doesn't know what they will think. He wonders what *Women's Wear Daily* will say in their review the next day. They've always been kind to him, enormously so. But it's 1983, not 1973; there are certain things he can't get away with anymore.

"There's champagne over there. I'm getting us some," says Steve.

"None for me, thank you," Andy says.

"I'll have his," Halston says. His mirrored sunglasses are back on and he has a palm placed against the small of Liza's back. Liza, Steve, and Andy are his supporters tonight. Since he began licensing his name to a series of products and fashion, he thought that his trust circle might grow. Soon, everyone would be looking out for his best interests. What's good for Halston is good for the Halston brand. It should be obvious. But it's not. And the circle has been shrinking.

He looks all around the great hall. He sees that they are standing underneath a giant blue whale that is suspended from the ceiling above them by a series of intricately arranged wires.

"If that whale came down on us right now, the artistic output of the entire city of New York City would be decimated," Halston says.

"If that thing fell on me, the portrait I just finished of Christina Onassis would increase in value by 5,000%," Andy says.

"Did you remember to sign it this time?" asks Liza. Halston laughs.

"No, I haven't yet as a matter of fact." Andy reddens, like a dead arm newly pumped with blood. "Making a mental note now."

"Liza, let's go to the bathroom," Halston says.

"Oh, yes. Let's," she answers quickly, putting out her cigarette in a nearby ashcan.

"Where are they going?" Halston hears Steve ask Andy as he and Liza are moving away. He has returned with flutes and a whole bottle of Dom Perignon.

"I think Halston is going to sew a rip in Liza's dress," Andy answers, exhaling a funnel of smoke.

It's a single bathroom with a lock. As soon as they're both inside, Halston dumps an amber vial out onto the ledge of the black Duravit sink and arranges the coke into a pair of long, sharp lines. Stripes, he thinks, seeing the fine white lines against the black surface. He should've added stripes to the JCPenney collection. Vertical stripes. Or beaded stripes. Or. Just stripes.

"Look, someone left a present for me," Liza says picking up a flute of champagne resting on the sink next to the soap dispenser. "You can't take me anywhere." She does a series of twirls inside the bathroom, the golden edges of her gown fluttering up like the spun gold of Rumplestiltskin. The harsh, overhead lights illuminate the sweat on her forehead and on her upper lip. She is bubbling, a bit manic, laughing. Like a tall puppet. "Well, except here. Right here. You can take me right. Here," she says poking his forehead with her index finger, her nail painted smaragd green.

He remembers how Liza was when he first met her, how horrible she felt about her body. She thought she had no elegance, or grace, or style. She hated that she was a little too hairy for a woman. She was an ugly duckling with a good voice and a famous mother, that's how she saw herself. She didn't even own luggage and she had very little money. Halston told her to go out and buy a set of Louis Vuitton luggage.

"You're going to faint at how expensive it is, but I want you to buy what you can afford and have it sent to me," he told her.

Three weeks later, she came to pick up the luggage and Halston had filled it with clothes he had made for her. It was an entire wardrobe. He made her everything she would need, clothes for every occasion. He even made a leather-bound look-book for her which showed how to accessorize each outfit and when and how to wear it. They were clothes that accentuated her best and hid her worst. Liza had wonderful shoulders and great legs, and he wanted to highlight them. She was gamine and wore bold colors well. Liza made his clothes come alive.

Liza always makes him feel better about himself. Better than he is alone. Halston loves her so much in this moment. He wants to tell her, but it comes out a different way. It's all about him. He can't find a way to make it about her.

"I really need you here with me tonight, Liza," he says. He is momentarily frightened.

"You have me. I'm right here." She bends down to do one of the lines.

"If I'm not blitzed when those models come down the runway and something bad happens, then I'm going to be very upset."

"Don't worry. It's going to be great, Halston." She kisses him on the lips, and he tastes the cocaine and the sweet and sour mix of champagne and lip gloss. "And, if it's not great, we'll just torch this whole fucking place down and everyone inside of it." Halston smiles. He does the other line and at the end of it, he looks up at the mirror. Liza leans her head toward him, and they both look at themselves in the mirror. Halston and Liza. He wants to remember this moment. They both smile, kind half-smiles. Then they burst out laughing.

The lights dim briefly as if it's intermission during one of her musicals.

"Let's go open this show, goddamnit!" Liza says, already on her way out the door.

Everyone has begun to take their seats. Liza sits down next to Steve and Andy and places her gold Art Deco clutch on the empty seat next to her.

Someone hands Halston a microphone. He looks out over the sea of people who have assembled to celebrate his new line. To celebrate him. Or this new version of him, whoever that is. There are coordinated parties happening in several different cities around the country at this exact moment—Chicago, L.A. Miami, Washington D.C. It's like the whole country is waiting for him to address them. He is standing directly underneath the belly of the whale.

"You know me, I'm as American as apple pie," he begins. "I'm the original Mr. Sweater Set. I like casual clothes and have never been able to make them. When I was a kid, I always shopped at Penney's. Remember, I come from Des Moines, Iowa." The audience laughs, and he takes the opportunity to look up for a second before continuing his speech. It's like the whale is cresting the surface of the water before plunging back down.

"What you are about to see, ladies and gentlemen, is the most challenging and gratifying fashion job I have ever done. This is for the American people," he says. "Over half of America goes into JCPenney at some point. When I think of these clothes, I think of my family. I have a sister in Little Rock and a sister-in-law in Gainesville, Florida, and they're dying for these clothes to come out." He pauses and strikes a lanky pose. "Who needs cashmere?"

"Why doesn't he just send his sisters the clothes? Why do they have to go to JCPenney?" he can see Steve mouthing to Liza. At least that's what he imagines Steve is saying. The lights in the great hall dim except for tracking lights that illuminate the great blue whale. Beneath it, the runway floor lights up from below, and a shimmering effect provided by the sheer aqua iridescence of the whale makes the whole hall appear as if it's underwater. We are now all submerged, Halston thinks. We are all the rich people on the Titanic who didn't get off in time.

He takes his seat next to Liza just as "Let's Dance" by David Bowie comes on over the speaker and the Halstonettes begin to come out one by one. A polyester crepe print blouse with tiny H's along the neckline; a casual sundress accessorized with a silver Elsa Perretti bean; a herringbone tweed skirt paired with a crème cowl-neck sweater; a white Memorial Day-inspired half-pant with a khaki tank top and a Halstonette cheerfully waving a small American flag; a melton wrap coat with contrasting edges; a printed canvas knit shirtdress with self-sash, topped off with a single-breasted coat in taupe wool; a red marabou jacket; an ivory matte jersey with more tiny H's; and then, finally, his showstopper: lightweight Shetland wool separates—a stole, wrapped over a matching sweater, and a knitted dress.

Halston looks up again at the blue whale just as the showstopper comes to the end of the runway. How far did the whale have to travel? How many miles, how many leagues through the ocean must it have traversed to end up right here, floating in air?

When they pull up to Studio 54, there's a predictable crowd surrounding the door. It's not as big of a crowd as it used to be four or five years ago, but it's still no cakewalk to get into the place and that's what Halston likes most about it. If you're not famous then you better be extremely good-looking, wearing something extraordinary, or someone worth screwing. You better be fucking fabulous, or you best get out of his way.

He once saw a man in line dressed in drag as Mrs. Danvers from the movie *Rebecca*. The drag queen was standing next to a Joan Fontaine doppelgänger, complete with makeup that made both of them appear as if they were in an old black-and-white movie. They both so enraptured Halston that he thought about doing an entire Halston Originals collection based around the look. But then he must have forgotten about it or he became caught up in something else. He always has so many projects running at the same time. He could still put out that collection if he wanted to. He could have the Halstonettes walk down the runway in vintage-inspired gowns and gray makeup at Olympic Tower. He could resurrect an entire forgotten era of glamour and elegance if he wanted to. It would be the antithesis of anything you could ever find at a JCPenney. He is still the standard bearer in the industry. That moniker has not, and can never be, sold.

He takes a long drag and ashes his cigarette before finally putting it out in the ashtray in the limo door. He feels for the mirrored sunglasses in the side pocket of his black sports jacket. He only started wearing the sunglasses so that people couldn't see how bloodshot his eyes were. But there are only friends in this limo—they're allowed to see who he really is. Roy Halston Frowick from Des Moines. The Hatmaker from the Midwest. The Haute Courtier of Seventh Avenue. The King of Olympic Tower. The Prince of Powder. The Mayor of Studio 54. Liza Minnelli's Best Friend. Andy Warhol's Muse. Steve Rubell's Favorite Celebrity. The Man Standing Beneath a Giant Whale. Halston. Simply Halston.

"Oh look, it's Faye Dunaway," says Andy, pointing out of the tinted window of the limo before doing a bump offered by Steve.

"Who cares? Look at that fine specimen over there," Halston says, pointing to a tall black man in a red windbreaker, white jeans, and hi-tops. "Steve, why don't you get out and go let him into the club?" Halston has always preferred black rough trade.

"Just because you sell in malls now doesn't mean I'm gonna start letting in bridge-and-tunnel," Steve says. Halston rolls his eyes and puts his sunglasses back on. Liza grabs onto his shoulders and looks him dead-on. He thinks she might be trying to steady him before they exit the limo, so he doesn't erupt at Steve in public. She has always been able to sense when he needs to be calmed down. But then he realizes that she's just using his mirrored sunglasses to quickly fix her hair.

When Studio 54 reopened after Steve and his business partner, Ian, got out of prison (having served time for tax evasion), Halston offered to throw a dinner gala to celebrate his return. Steve told him that he would prefer it if Calvin Klein threw the dinner. Calvin Klein, not him. It was practically unforgivable. To Halston, Steve is that ugly kid in high school the popular people keep around for entertainment. The kid who is always one bad night away from getting kicked out of the clique. And Halston has always been the leader of the clique. Steve would do well to remember that.

Steve moves the rope aside so that Halston, Liza, and Andy can pass through.

"Is Margaux here tonight? I didn't see her at the

show," Liza asks Andy. Andy does a weird shake of his head that isn't quite a no or a yes.

Liza gives Mark, the doorman, a kiss as they walk past him. "I love you!" she says. Liza is positively lit. She links arms with Halston and they walk in together.

Halston is surrounded by the familiar wall of mirrors that make up the front vestibule of the club. The mirrors are on all sides of him, including the ceiling. Some are faded at the corners of the panes as if they are slowly reverting into glass. He sees small cracks in them like spider webs that appear in one's field of vision and then disappear the moment they are noticed, having melted onto warm skin. He imagines what it must have been like to enter the club back when it was an opera house in the Roaring Twenties, a period by which he has always been fascinated, slightly jealous that he could not have lived then instead. He can feel the ghosts of past patrons staring back at him, superimposing their faces over his reflection. They stare back at him through his own eyes, reflecting back to him the optimism of another time. Old faces that look like new faces. A parade of faces.

As they enter the main floor, the pulse of the club hits Halston like an electrical charge. It jolts him back to the present. He is home now, and he feels a bit better. 54 is home, just like 101. He doesn't have to be anyone here. Here is exactly who he is. Whoever he is, he is here. No one is after him to reinvent himself or borrow his name to sell a piece of luggage, or an umbrella, or ask him for a check. Here he is alright. He feels so safe and sure of himself all of a sudden that he never wants to leave 54. And even if he didn't, who would ever make him?

Patrice Rushen's "Haven't You Heard?" is playing as Halston makes his way over to the DJ booth. "Liza, come with me," he says taking her by the hand and leading her up a small staircase to the booth. It seems to him in this instant of having done this countless enough times he actually owns this small piece of the club. This real estate is his.

"Let's do another line—I love this song!" Liza says. She flips over a small drink ledge that has a mirror on the opposite side (Steve really does think of everything) and then pulls the amber vial out of her clutch and dumps out what's left.

"The show was a complete success. You know that, don't you? Oh, I hope you do. I really do," Liza says to him. He does know. He could tell after it was over. He saw one fashion reporter give him a nod right after the show that seemed to say, "Is it possible that you've done it again? Can I believe what I've seen here tonight?" Halston does half the line and leaves the rest for Liza.

"Liza's right, Halston. It was a success," Andy says, joining them in the booth. "You shined. Everything really came together." Andy uptalks, but it's endearing.

"Is there even a JCPenney in New York City?" asks Steve who Halston has failed to notice joining them in the DJ booth. Andy and Liza both look at each other like they can't quite comprehend the question. Like, it's in a language that neither of them can understand. In fact, there *isn't* a JCPenney in New York City. The closest one is in Paramus, New Jersey. Halston knows this but was hoping that other people wouldn't care or might have forgotten. And he never imagined anyone would dare mention it to him. The department store that is selling clothes which bear his name doesn't even have a store in the city he has called home for twenty-six years. It embarrasses him.

"You know, Steve Rubell, sometimes you're just too fucking Jewish. Even for New York," says Halston. He pronounces Steve's last name like it's an incurable venereal disease.

Halston steps out of the booth and walks out into the mass of people that have gathered on the dance floor, cresting like waves with the rhythm of the music. He wants to be swallowed up in it. Swallowed up whole by them. "He's the Greatest Dancer" by Sister Sledge comes on. Of course. It's the song that mentions him in its lyrics.

When the song used to come on at work, he would make everyone stop what they were doing until his name had passed. But he hasn't heard it in a couple of years and it almost sneaks up on him when he hears his name again. He looks toward the DJ booth and sees Steve who has his arm around the DJ, looking back at him.

It's a Tuesday night, and there are mostly younger

people in the club. Their images reflect back at him from a mirrored disco ball that spins above—another parade of faces. The pieces of the mirror in the ball reflect lights onto the dance floor and illuminate people for a flash before rotating and moving on. He suddenly spies Truman Capote near the center and nods in his direction, but Truman doesn't notice. Truman is dancing with a shirtless Italian man. Although Halston can hardly call what Truman is doing "dancing," it's more like creepily prancing around the man in a predatory prowl, encircling him with gusto and beet-faced bravado, too drunk to be any threat, too bold to be outright ignored. The Italian man's sweaty chest hair has caught the lights in just the right way so that he glistens. Halston would dress him in something light, a white linen suit perhaps with tan loafers and a neutral suede belt. He might trim the unruly mustache but keep the chest hair as it is, allowing its downy ringlets to pop out over the collar of a pale blue cotton shirt with buttons made of mother-of-pearl.

Someone comes up from behind and caresses his shoulder with a familiar touch. It's Liza. And although they never do it, tonight he thinks they will dance.

Don't Stop Me Now

With the sound off, the television in Freddie's hotel room played an episode of *The Golden Girls* in the background while they improvised their own dialogue. Kenny was Blanche, Cleo was Rose, Diana was Dorothy, and Freddie was Sophia.

"What are you bitches doing in here?" Freddie (as Sophia) said as, on the screen, Estelle Getty burst into the kitchen to discover the three other ladies sharing a cheesecake.

"Group sex," said Cleo (as Rose). "And we need more tops."

"Don't forget the lube, honey. You know how dry I get!" said Kenny in a drawl. He got up from his seat and started to mimic Blanche sashaying over to the refrigerator in a fur-lined silk calico robe.

"We know, Blanche. I think everyone knows," said Diana in her best Dorothy Zbornak.

They all erupted into hysterics. Diana was giggling on the sofa. "So, what are you all doing tonight?"

"We're going to Royal Vauxhall Tavern," said Freddie.

"I've never heard of it. I'd like to come," said Diana.

Freddie, Cleo, and Kenny all acted surprised that she had even suggested it and tried to dissuade her, but they all quickly climbed on board just as Diana knew they would. She was feeling mischievous that evening; there would be no talking her out of anything.

"Well, you can't go as you to the club. We'll have to disguise you somehow," said Cleo.

"I think I might have an idea," Diana said. She announced her plan.

"This is going to be bloody brilliant!" said Freddie. He was still pumped up from that night's show at Covent Garden and was really jazzed about her plan. It almost sounded like the opening of a joke: *So a princess in drag walks into a gay bar and orders a drink …* "What a delicious idea!" Freddie thought it was everything. If they could pull it off, Diana knew they'd be telling this story for years.

"I just love it," Cleo said.

"I have the perfect pair of skinny jeans for you to wear," Freddie offered. "They're fabulous. Let's get you dressed, Butch."

"Do you really think this will work?" Diana asked, her voice kind of quiet but with that hint of excitement.

"You're a princess, and I'm a queen. Honey, this is *so* happening."

The plan was simple: they'd make the world's most famous woman—a veritable icon—pass for an eccentric male model. Why not? It was worth a shot. Diana never got to go out, especially to the gay clubs with Freddie when he'd blow into town. Lately she hadn't gone out at all. Freddie had gotten to calling her "Rapunzel"—"Oh, Rapunzel, Rapunzel, let down your hair!"

"It's not that bad, Freddie," Diana said.

"Let's execute your escape then."

Diana had been listening to Queen since before she could remember. Certainly before Charles and the boys. Maybe even since West Heath. "Fat Bottomed Girls" had been an early standard, but "Don't Stop Me Now" was her all-time favorite, and Freddie and the boys had sung it that night at Covent Garden just for her. She and a handler had watched the band from a private balcony. Then the four of them fell into Freddie's black town car, which waited at the exit of the auditorium.

Cleo and Kenny were both comics whom Freddie had introduced her to a few years earlier. Diana had gotten rid of her handler for a couple hours, convincing him that she could take care of herself after the concert. She wasn't expected to be anywhere else that night; Charles was in Balmoral, and the boys were both in bed.

There had been no paparazzi stalking her in London for this jaunt. It had been leaked to the papers two days before that she was en route to Swaziland on a goodwill tour. She'd go of course, just not that week. This is what it took to have a life: fake itineraries, large sunglasses, escaping through secret exit doors.

She wasn't really shy; that was an image created by the media. She was just careful about who she gave herself to. She had to be. To the ones she loved, she was never shy. She was fearless. And she let her friends have as much of her as they wanted.

"Let's slick your hair back with pomade," Cleo said, rubbing the gel between her palms and tamping down Diana's beautiful hair.

"You look like a twink! I love this!" Freddie proclaimed. He grabbed the pomade and flattened the sides of his own hair. He'd lost so much on top recently that there was nothing really left worth teasing. "I'd fuck you," he told Diana.

Cleo stopped zhuzhing Diana's hair. "Language, Freddie! You're speaking to royalty."

"Excuse me, Cleo. I'd fuck you, Your Highness," he said.

"Really?" Diana asked. Her blue eyes twinkled at him from her reflection in the mirror. "You would?"

"Honey, you look better in those jeans than I ever have. That's a fact. I mean, check out that ass."

Kenny pulled out one of Freddie's many army jackets. "How about this?" It was structured in just that way. Fashion had so many angles now. All bold colors and planked shoulder lines. You could lose an eye on an exposed shoulder blade in 1988.

"Here, and this too." Cleo placed a cap askew on Diana's head.

"Put these on," said Freddie, handing over a pair of aviator sunglasses.

By the time they were done with her, they had transformed her into a beautiful gent—slightly affected. Vapid even. Could easily pass for a male model, especially with her height and athletic build. Diana gazed into the mirror and lost herself for a bit. She was easily recognizable to herself. But then again she was also the very picture of her secondary school self: those couple of years when she'd eschewed dresses and frills and started to dress more comfortably. Back then her brother had even confessed to her that he thought she was looking a bit lesbian.

When they arrived at the Royal Vauxhall Tavern in South London, Freddie got out of the town car and started hamming it up for the crowd of young men waiting behind velvet ropes to enter the club. His distraction allowed Diana to slip inside unnoticed.

"This is so *Roman Holiday*!" Kenny said as they made their way inside.

Diana sauntered up to the bar. "What can I get ya, mate?" asked the bartender. He looked a bit like Sid Vicious, Diana thought.

"A glass of white wine, please," she said in the deepest voice she could muster.

"Here ya go. That'll be one pound sixty."

It worked! I can't bloody believe it worked, Diana thought just as she realized she had no money; she hadn't carried any in years.

"I got it for you," Cleo said, handing over a fiver. She winked at Diana, and the two of them were sucked into the crowd.

The boys around her were hopping up and down to Erasure. She loved this. It had been years since she'd been out like this, among the real people of London. She couldn't believe it was working. No one seemed to recognize her at all. No paparazzi or cameras flashing in her face. Unreal.

She took a sip of wine and looked out onto the crowd. Gay men had always treated her kindly. They seemed to sense how difficult it was to be trapped in something and not know a way out. Not that she wanted a "way out" necessarily. She would never leave William and Harry, but her marriage to Charles had been much more than she had bargained for. She had watched a tape of their wedding once and almost had a panic attack. The world was watching her. It would always be watching her.

"Hey there, mate. You doing anything later?" purred an older gentleman in faded denim. He was sizing her up.

"Beat it, babe. He's with me tonight," Kenny said, coming to her rescue. "He was trying to pick you up!" he said into Diana's ear, over the din of the music.

"Well, I would certainly hope so!" Diana answered. "Where's Freddie?"

"Over there. Look," said Cleo, pointing toward Freddie at the center of a sweaty pile of young men. He had already stripped down to a white tank top; rivulets of perspiration poured down his face.

Freddie from the planet Mercury. Her Freddie. He got her. He knew what it was like. But, then again, he loved the attention. Just lapped it up. All the lovers he'd told her about—all those men, the occasional woman. She worried about him. She didn't ask about his health, but she had noticed he was looking thinner, his cheeks more sunken, his skin color sallow. She didn't ask him directly, but she'd definitely seen all that before. The men she'd visited in hospital, their hands like dry corpses. She remembered them looking up at her with milky, almost blind eyes, grateful for the human contact. People needed to be touched. It was a need like water. The look in their eyes. She never could forget it.

Freddie loved her, though. He understood the real Diana, the one the cameras could never catch.

"Gather around, ladies and gentlemen! It's Wednesday night, and you know what that means!" screamed a drag queen in a beehive wig and a blue sparkly dress. His accent was Cockney, his voice almost ridiculously deep.

"Wednesdays. Are. A. *Draaaaggggg!*" screamed back the audience.

"That's right, pets. And tonight's a special night because all our contestants are paying homage to famous people or characters. First up, ooooh, lookie lookie, boys, there's Glenn Close in *Fatal Attraction*!"

Out walked a gorgeous man done up in Alex Forrest's white power suit, the one she is wearing when she and Michael Douglas have drinks before getting caught in the rain. Her leonine blond wig was perfectly crimped to match Close's in the film, and she carried a stuffed bunny by its ears. Diana and Charles had seen a cut of the movie after its London premiere once the deafening buzz from the States had catapulted its way across the pond. She recalled feeling sorry for the character when the audience clearly had been directed to hate her in the most vicious way.

"Don't get in her way, or she'll boil your bunny, you little faggots!" growled the hostess into the microphone.

"Next up, another import from across the pond: Melanie Griffith!"

Drag Melanie was wearing a facsimile of her *Working Girl* dress, the one she sports when Tess McGill first meets Harrison Ford's character. The drag queen was wearing a wig that was too orange, though. It made her look like a carrot. Diana couldn't help laughing a little.

"And now for a hometown favorite. She's larger than life and more well-known than any character in any movie. Drop to your knees to hail the great one, boys.

It's ... Diana, Princess of Wales!"

A drag queen wore an imitation version of the white beaded gown with matching bolero Diana had worn to the British Fashion Awards at Albert Hall—the dress Catherine Walker had designed for her. It was the night she had donned a crown on the red carpet. The People's Princess.

"Oh, babe, look. Oh, my God," Kenny whispered in her ear.

"Just one more minute. We have to stay a little longer," she said. She looked Freddie's way and caught his eye. He opened his wide mouth in surprise and put up his open palm to it. The men started to cheer for her on stage. Well, not her, but the drag queen who looked like her.

"We love you, Di!"

"Oh, God, I'm dying. I'm dying!" said an older man next to her, wearing black jeans and a Smiths t-shirt. He looked like he was about to faint.

"Long live Princess Di!" The drag queen playing her did a royal kind of wave, one Diana herself had performed many times in the past. The performer pulled up her dress a little to affect a curtsy, somehow low enough to the floor so that Diana could see the pectorals underneath the bodice of the gown.

Everyone clapped. And hollered. And she did too. She handed her empty wineglass to Cleo and started clapping right along with them.

"This one, huh?" said the hostess. She had placed her hand over the Princess Diana drag queen's head. The cheering grew louder and louder. Diana reached for the cap she was wearing and pulled it down farther in an attempt to hide her smile, which she knew she couldn't possibly hide for long. She nodded to Cleo and Kenny, and they alerted Freddie, who stood closer to the stage. The trio quickly exited the club with Diana following close in their wake.

As she made her way out, Diana noticed the exterior of the club looked like the outside of the Colosseum in Rome, its middle section lit up to attract revelers from all roads that led to its doors.

Freddie peered over at her in the backseat of the car and smiled, knocking the cap off her head and petting her hair, which was still thick with pomade.

"That was wonderful, Freddie," she said. "Thank you."

"No, thank you, Princess," he answered, leaning against her.

As they drove away from the club, Diana gazed out the car window. She thought about the drag queen back in his dressing room so easily removing the props that had allowed him to become her for the night: the gown, the tiara, the blond wig. She herself could not do the same, of course. She could never take off Princess Diana. Like a child at Halloween, a costume can be really fun for a day, but being dressed as a pirate or a princess and keeping up the act all the time—it was exhausting.

She knew they had to leave the club when they did. As good as the drag queen had been, she knew no one could do her as well as she could do herself. And the world, not just drag queens, needed her. Freddie needed her. Those dying young men alone in their beds needed her. Her boys. Even Charles. The world needed her. Nothing could stop her.

Charlie Movie Star

When Rock used to look in the mirror during his Charlie Movie Star days, he would never deny the fact that he was handsome. Handsome men know they're handsome. There was no reason to be coy or overly modest about it—that kind of thing just reeked of phoniness to him.

He used to have the kind of black hair that was almost blue like Clark Kent's in the old Superman comics he read as a boy back in Winnetka. His strong, square jaw, a built upper chest, that mythical "V" shape of his torso—he had all the right things that make a man real, topped off with a face the camera adored. He loved being seen as a real man. And, my God, he had charisma. That went a long way toward enhancing his purely physical features. That easy, casual way about him that had always opened doors leading to an easier path through life—it's not something you can fake, even in Hollywood.

Before arriving at the White House that night, Rock searched for those same things in the bathroom mirror in his suite at the Mayflower Hotel. It had become a habit of his. Whenever he'd catch his reflection somewhere—passing by a shop window, staring into a photographer's camera lens—he would pause to see if he could locate that younger man he had once been, the one in all the movies. At fifty-nine years old, that man was becoming harder to find. His hair was all gray, not black and certainly not blue. His face was lined with deep, unforgiving crevasses etched down his cheeks, hugging the corners of his mouth—deep enough for him to run credit cards through if he wanted. He supposed he was still what some would consider handsome (heck, that whole distinguished dad look had definitely secured for him the part on *The Devlin Connection* even though the show had flopped spectacularly), but now it was an older and more weathered kind of handsome. Gawking rather than being gawked at. He wasn't used to it. Not at all.

Ron and Nancy had invited him to the White House to attend the State Dinner for President Miguel de la Madrid Hurtado of Mexico. This was something he'd done once before during Ron's first administration, and it had been a good time, but also a surprising one. He wasn't particularly close with the President but they had become friendly at several Hollywood functions in the past. When he came to Washington this time, he'd considered accepting their invitation to stay at the

White House, but had opted for the Mayflower on a recommendation from his secretary.

During his first visit, staying at the White House had presented its own unique set of problems that went along with the more obvious perks. He'd hated having to check in at the security hut like a damn tourist, for example. Back in Hollywood at the Universal lot, he had always simply waved a hand from his car at one of the security guards and they'd let him pass. They would never have stopped him at the gate to check his driver's license. Rock Hudson—Movie Star? It would've been unheard of.

There were also things at the White House that remained invisible to the average straight male visitor, yet appeared to Rock as temptations flashing at him around every corner. They were as obvious to him as a dead trick floating in a Beverly Hills swimming pool on a Sunday morning. Along the hallway of the East Wing, Secret Service stood at regular intervals at every third door. As Rock walked past them, he was reminded of his late night hauntings of Flex, the L.A. bathhouse he often frequented. There too, men stood guard in front of their rooms. They had towels wrapped around their slim waists that were slightly opened up at the crotch as if to invite him in. Some of the men appeared to him as stoic and impenetrable as these Secret Service members—without affect, robotic and vacant, as if it were up to Rock to tell them how they should want him. Turning them on might be as easy as caressing the small soft place under the chin to flip a switch. Others appeared to him starved, their desires or kinks on full display. Those were the men who were hungry for any kind of male touch, any kind of sustenance Rock could always be depended upon to give.

There were also gangs of young interns who had been seemingly let loose to roam about the White House unchaperoned, all with their pretty little ambitions, their awe at the sudden proximity to power, those hormonal hailstorms percolating. He'd once slipped directions to his room into the pocket of one of them in a moment of uncharacteristic indiscretion, convinced that the boy (he had thought of him at first as a "boy," but the young man must've been at least twenty-one, college-aged) had made a certain eye signal with which he was very familiar. In fact, the young man had made eyes at him at several points during the evening and Rock felt certain that he could get him into bed without a lot of coaxing. He was, after all, Hollywood royalty.

The boy came to his room later that night. Rock let him in and began rubbing him through his pants, feeling him grow hard. The boy (who gave the name Thomas after some initial hesitation) was simply beautiful, exactly Rock's type: blond, blue-eyed, young, well-built. This set of criteria was well known to those in his trusted circle back home and his friends would often make sure to invite young men who fit this type to his pool parties. He usually liked them taller but he wasn't as choosy as he had once been and Thomas was a specimen at which anyone would have marveled, no matter his height. He let Rock undress him and because he was so much shorter, it was easy to pick him up and take him to the bed, laying him on top of the duvet in such a way that his body naturally arched back against one of several oblong, tasseled pillows under his bare back. As they fucked, Rock could feel Thomas gripping his shoulder tightly at first as if he were in pain and wanted Rock to slow down. But then he cupped one hand on Rock's buttock and pulled him in closer, all the way. Rock kissed him deeply and felt, in that moment, as connected to Thomas as he had with any actor in any scene in any movie in which he'd ever appeared.

The White House never seemed cozy or intimate to him. It felt more like a well-kept museum than the actual home of anyone, much less the President of the United States. It wasn't even that big, he thought. Tab Hunter's house was bigger.

"Rock, dear, we're so glad you could come," the First Lady said to him.

"Hi!" he responded, at first. "Thank you so much, ma'am."

"We're old friends. You can dispense with the formalities."

"In that case, you look incredible, Nancy," he said, flashing a smile. Rock remembered that Nancy Reagan (née Davis) had been known back in the day as the "MGM Blowjob Queen." He really couldn't judge anyone though. There had been one married producer who he'd let blow him occasionally back in the early days of his career and that man turned out to be a very good friend to have in his back pocket. He might have even saved Rock's career once.

"You're so kind. Charming as ever," said Nancy.

"Have you got me seated next to someone special?" Rock asked.

"Every guest of ours is special! You know that," she said. "You'll be seated at my table."

"Wonderful. I'm honored."

"Rock, you're too thin. We need to fatten you up," she said, gripping his shoulder in a friendly gesture.

"You're thin, also," he said. Nancy nodded and smiled. "I think I caught a flu bug while I was filming in Israel, but I'm feeling fine now."

Rock had worked with the President's first wife, Jane Wyman, on a couple of films in the '50s. The first film they did together was *Magnificent Obsession*. He'd caught an airing of it after Carson one night a couple months back. Not having seen it in years, he settled back and found himself utterly absorbed by it. He followed the story very closely, wondering if he'd ever seen the whole movie in its entirety. He wasn't actually sure.

He must have at one point. Back home at the Castle he kept videocassettes of all his movies and many of his favorites.

In *Magnificent Obsession*, he played a rich, swaggering playboy named Bob Merrick whose recklessness gets him in a boating accident which inadvertently causes a doctor to die when the doctor's own resuscitator, commandeered to save Merrick's life, is missing at the precise moment the doctor himself needs it. Later, Merrick is also responsible for accidentally blinding the doctor's widow, Helen Phillips, played by Wyman. Merrick then goes to medical school to become a doctor so he can cure her blindness.

"Didn't Jane Wyman already play blind?" asked Jack Navaar, his boyfriend at the time, as he thumbed through Rock's script.

"She was deaf in *Johnny Belinda*. Not blind."

"Now she's playing blind? This is such trash," said Jack. "Joan Crawford already did that whole blind thing last year in *Torch Song*."

"It's melodramatic." Rock had responded. "But it's still one helluva part."

"I think Jane won an Oscar for playing that deaf-mute," Jack said.

Rock made a spiraling sign with his finger and said, "Whoopee." He stood up, towering over Jack with his hands on his waist. "I could win an Oscar, too."

Jane Wyman had been very kind to him on set. It

was one of his first starring roles and Rock had been so nervous that some of his scenes had to be reshot thirty or forty times. Jane had been so patient and professional, just a lovely person. He was so appreciative that he asked her later why she was being so nice to him. "Let me tell you something, Rock." She took his hand and said very confidentially, "It was handed to me by somebody. And I handed it to you. And now it's your turn to hand it to somebody else."

At the premiere of *Magnificent Obsession* at the Westwood Theater, the studio had made him bring a gal named Betty Abbott to the premiere and Jack came with a young actress named Claudia Boyer. That's just what he had to do back then. He would never have been able to arrive with Jack or even make eyes at him at the premiere. He'd wanted to though. He would love to have shared that moment with him, watching his big break happen on the screen with his man sitting right next to him. In the lobby he had tapped Jack on the shoulder "1-2-3," their code for "I love you."

One of the things that struck him while watching the movie all these years later was how easygoing he appeared on the screen. Affable and approachable. Flirtatious and strapping. Overtly, almost chronically heterosexual. A regular "Charlie Movie Star." That's the name he came up for himself during that period of his life his friends had called the "Impossible Years" when he'd been a real marquee idol and maybe a little bit full of himself. But there had been so much more going on beneath his exterior that the Joe Meatloaf and Suzy Chapstick theatergoers would never have seen themselves. His face hadn't been marked yet with any of it. It had always been such a dependable mask.

"Rock, let's get a picture of the three of us," said President Reagan, motioning to the White House photographer.

"I'd be honored, Mr. President," he said. Nancy stood between them in her bright red dress. She clasped Rock's hand and hooked her other arm through the President's.

"Smile!" the photographer said. Flash.

The cab driver looked at him oddly in the rearview mirror when he gave the address in the Southeast neighborhood of Navy Yard.

"Sure you want to go there, sir? It's not a good neighborhood. Lots of crime. And it's tough to get a cab back."

"I think I can manage, but thanks," Rock said.

Rock had heard about Tracks from an ex-lover who had been there a couple months before when it first opened. He said there had been several Marines who'd come down to the Navy Yard from the Marine Barracks on Eighth Street and ended up at Tracks the night he'd been there. Rock imagined them just like he had been back in the day when he was fresh off his own time in the service. Most of them would probably pretend that they were unaware of the bar's gay reputation. His ex-lover had also given him the address of a nearby townhouse in Capitol Hill that operated as a no-questions-asked private sex club. But Rock had learned the hard way not to put himself in situations like that and thought he'd try his luck out at Tracks.

When he first walked in, he was cautious by habit. Back in the day, he would never have just waltzed into a sissy bar like this. Maybe if he'd gone with his publicist (who had also been his live-in lover at the time) he wouldn't have cared. No one really knew about that kind of thing and it was easy to just hide in plain sight. But it would've been a very rare event. He much preferred to have friends over to the Castle for drinks and dinner. Only in the last couple of years had he allowed himself to be seen in a gay establishment at all. Before his relationship with Marc Christian had deteriorated, he'd started going out to gay bars and restaurants in West Hollywood with Marc because Marc liked them so much.

But he was older now and wasn't as easily recognized. It was perhaps the one good thing about losing his looks. Older gay men fade into the background. At least he thought they did—he certainly never saw them. Sometimes he thought about the older man back in Winnetka who used to pay Rock to blow him in the back of his convenience store. Surely that man was dead by now. Or he'd be close to a hundred years old. He wondered where old homosexuals went. What happened to them? He had never asked any of his friends and thought now that he probably should have.

The crowd at Tracks was very young. So many of the kind he liked too. They were young and confident and bopping around almost in unison. He didn't recognize the song playing and he also couldn't tell if a man or a woman was the singer. He wasn't sure that something like that mattered now.

After ordering a glass of gin, he wandered into an outdoor courtyard that turned out to be a beach volleyball court. There was a hamburger and hotdog grille in the corner adjacent to a series of banked wooden steps on one side for people to hang out and watch the game. Several shirtless young men were currently engaged in one. They went diving for the ball, grunting and hollering. It reminded Rock of being on the beach back home with friends and horsing around. He loved being surrounded by all those wonderful young men he used to have at his parties.

One of them came over to him with his shirt slung over his shoulder, all sweaty with a dewy sheen on his stomach. He was very attractive, perhaps mid-twenties. He was also exactly Rock's type: blond, blue-eyed, well-built, and young. He gave off a vibe as if he'd be just as comfortable with a woman as he would a man—Rock's kind of guy.

"Hiya! Some game going here, huh?" Rock asked him.

"Yeah, I guess," he said. "You should join."

"I'd just beat you all and what fun would that be?" Rock answered.

"Oh yeah? I just bet you would." Rock wasn't sure if he was serious but he thought he caught a wink. "I'm Gus."

"Pleased to meet you, Gus." Rock put his hand out and Gus accepted it. "I'm—"

"Wait, hold on. Don't say it. I know exactly who you are."

"Really?" Rock said and looked away toward the game.

"Yes, I do. You're fucking Rock Hudson."

"Ya know me?" Rock got excited. He'd been out with Marc and his friends Mitch and George one night the month before, and their waiter had tried to stick them at a table near the kitchen and remained completely stone-faced when Mitch told him who Rock was. It had really bothered him.

"Yes, of course, I know you! I watched *All That Heaven Allows* when I was younger and it really hit me. The one where Jane Wyman is a rich widow and you're her gardener?"

"Landscape designer. Yes, I always liked that one. Jane certainly played a lot of widows back then," said Rock. He thought it was cute how Gus had provided

41

him a mini plot summary of the movie as if Rock might've forgotten it. Maybe he looked like he might not remember things. There had been a German remake of the film about ten years ago, but he'd never seen it.

"When I saw it, I wanted you to hold me next to a fire in a cabin with you wearing that red flannel shirt, just like you did with her," he blurted out, then paused, nervous. "God, that sounds cheesy."

"No, it doesn't. Not to me," Rock said.

"I watched it with my aunt. I think she knew I was a fag right then and there." Rock put his gin down on the wooden step and asked Gus to join him on the main dance floor. He was so far out of his comfort range and he couldn't believe he was doing this. But he was.

Gus put his head on Rock's chest, a chest that wasn't as strong as it had once been, muscles beginning to wane, just barely there. But still. There he was in the middle of the dance floor with this young man embracing him like it was the most natural thing in the world. He thought about how proud Jack Navaar would've been of him. Jack had always hated how Rock hid him from view.

While they danced, Rock spied a young man across the dance floor who was very tall and very thin. He was wearing a bright green t-shirt that, coupled with his unkempt brown hair, made him look like Shaggy from *Scooby-Doo*. He was dancing with a shorter man in a tight shirt and a mustache and a fat woman stuffed into a Betty Boop dress. Shaggy was hooked up to an IV and moved it across the dance floor with him as if it were a waltz. It was kind of touching, he thought, the young man escorting his IV, his partner for the night while his two friends danced together next to him also in a pair. When he attempted to dip his IV, Shaggy began to fall and his male friend caught him and brought him back to the corner of the bar where the three of them camped out for the rest of the song.

It hadn't occurred to Rock what might be physically wrong with Shaggy until he spied a group move all the way to the other side of the dance floor to get away from him. It was such a swift migration—the group's movement syncopated, almost choreographed with the sudden shift in song—that anyone else might've missed it. But Rock had seen one of them give a terse nod to the two others as if to alert them of a hazard in their midst and then all three of them quickly danced away from Shaggy and Shaggy's two friends to the beat of the new song (another song that Rock failed to recognize, but one whose tempo was slow enough so that he and Gus could rock back and forth while holding each other close and still feel invisible).

Rock admired Shaggy in a way. He seemed so unapologetic about who he was, what he was and his friends were so acclimated to it. Rock didn't understand this whole AIDS thing. *Newsweek* had done a cover story about it in '83 the year before calling it "the health threat of the century." But there had been so many of those throughout history already—it was unclear to Rock what made this the big one. He himself didn't feel threatened by it, but this young thin man was proof that it was out there in the world. Nobody Rock had gone to bed with had come down with it as far as he knew. And he'd been having sex with men for decades, longer than Shaggy certainly. He should have been swept away in the first wave of deaths. He must be in the clear now. Poor kid, he thought. So young. He might have a chance to beat it. Rock had beaten so much through the years to get where he was. Kids had it so much easier these days.

Still, he couldn't help but notice a certain alignment of feelings he had. That becoming older had so naturally edged up against his loss of looks, his loss of coveted casting. His overall failure to be recognized in public. None of it was random—he really didn't look like himself, a daunting fact to accept when your entire profession had always depended on that recognition. He assumed, unwittingly, that the face he had now was always built into the one he had then—that the man he was now was the man he was always destined to be.

He pulled Gus closer to him, tighter. He ran his hand down Gus's back, pressing into his spine, guiding him along the dance floor.

"Would you like to come back to my hotel room?" he asked. He felt he knew what Gus's answer would be.

The Boy Who Lived Next to the Boy Next Door

When Kurt came down with the disease, there were three guys in our circle who were already in the advanced stages of it: Justin, Pat, and Colin, known around town as "The Three." It was late fall 1981. The Three were handsome, well-built guys who'd all gone to Middlebury College together. They had tight bodies. They had fresh faces. They were the boys next door. Someone like me was the boy who lived *next* to the boy next door, forever looking out my window at my beautiful neighbor. The Three were fucking gorgeous. Then they were fucking sick. Then they were fucking dead.

The Three were always so sweet that you couldn't even hate them for their extreme kind of beauty. I mean, the worst thing you could say about any one of them was that they were *too* good-looking, as if that were even a thing. Justin was known around the baths as "Angel Boy" for his "Jacob wrestling with the angel" kind of holy beauty—

dark curly hair, blue apocryphal eyes, and pectorals that looked like they'd been sculpted out of Italian marble. Pat could've been Tom Selleck's stand-in on *Magnum, P.I.* His mustache was so thick and his arms were Brawny paper towel massive. And Colin looked like Gary Ewing from *Knots Landing* who I'd had a huge crush on since the show had premiered two years earlier.

The Three were all staying in my rental at Fire Island during their last summer which was lucky for me because really attractive men are sort of like roaches but in the best possible way. Where there's one you can safely assume that there are five to ten more underneath him (sometimes literally underneath him, especially at The Pines).

I was lucky enough to have had sex with Justin when he first moved to New York in the spring of 1977. I'll never forget it. Pat and Colin graduated a semester after him and quickly followed him to the city, but he was pretty much solo when he first arrived. In my case, it was the old story of the hot new guy getting into town and not really knowing how hot he is, so he'll sleep with anyone at first. That's something that happens and it happened between us. Later, when we became good friends, we both pretended that it never happened which is a skill that gay men seem to hone from almost the second they become sexually active. But I certainly never forgot it. I could never forget him pumping away on top of me, his back like a smooth wide alabaster expanse that I had to grab onto, grasping for his fabled wings. I always wished that it might happen again some night when we were both drunk. But it never did.

When The Three got sick in the fall, it was I who came up with the theory that it must be some kind of virus that was only attacking good-looking guys. Hot Guy Flu, I called it. Ridiculous hypothesis, I know, but what else could it possibly be? Mine was as good of a theory as anyone else had come up with. Neither myself nor any of the other average-looking gay guys I knew had come down with it, let alone any of the wretched trolls that cruised in the dark, far away from park lampposts and streetlights. The newspapers were barely covering the story at all and when they did, it was buried twenty-five pages deep and was only referred to as a new mysterious "gay cancer." It felt to me like the world, already disgusted with the very idea of us, could now assign a term for the kind of depraved nuisance we had put upon them. They could now openly refer to the literal plague of homosexuality. I would never have referred to the disease so glibly as "Hot Guy Flu" if I knew just how serious it was all about to get and that Justin, Pat, Colin, and Kurt as well as many others after them, would all be dead within a few months.

At the time, I fancied myself an amateur fiction writer. I'd had one short story published in the March 1980 issue of *Christopher Street* and was working on a couple others. Kurt Porter was the kind of guy I most liked to write about back then: Midwestern hunks who'd been cast out of their hometowns by religious zealots. They would arrive in the city with canvas knapsacks slung over their big shoulders and an unquenchable thirst for cock and ass which would then lead them to the nearest bus station bathroom for quick relief before being spit out into the streets of New York to search for more. It was a variation on a familiar plot and theme, one I'd seen repeated in the pages of several gay novels of the period. But for me, when I wrote that kind of character, it was like I was able to inject myself into a gay male fantasia that was almost completely removed from my own experience. I could play out the lives of the beautiful untouchables, that legion of men that seemed to multiply every year throughout those glorious '70s and early '80s.

Kurt was simply in a different league than The Three. Kurt was hot on an almost international level. Men, women, children, dogs—they all stopped what they were doing in order to look at him. There was even an urban legend that a bus driver had failed to watch where he was going and drove right into a fountain near Sheridan Square in 1979 all because he had turned to stare at Kurt who'd been walking down the street on his way to the gym. So, yes, when Kurt got Hot Guy Flu, there was no question what was really happening. Without a doubt, it was only the hot men of New York City who were being infected. Exceptionally hot men—no one else.

Kurt's initial symptoms: at first, he became thinner. Nothing that was too noticeable on someone with his hulking body. In fact, in the beginning, the weight loss leaned him out in a way that only made him appear more attractive. But then his cheeks began to sink in too much. His bright blue eyes—those eyes that you would've done anything to find pointed in your direction not even a month ago—sank deeper and deeper into his face until they looked like someone had pushed them in with their thumbs. They were still that same bright denim blue, but now they were also blood-stained and kind of distant. Fearful and vacant.

The last person who saw Kurt, right before Christmas that same year he died, described him in purely Gothic terms. He was practically a ghost, they said. Sitting alone on the subway, staring straight ahead at his own terrible reflection in the window of the train-car. He was barely recognizable. A hushed whisper of the beautiful man he'd once been.

But what was it that made the better looking people more susceptible to the virus?

"It's the pheromones. The virus is somehow attracted to their very special pheromones," said Doyle at a small gathering he was having in his apartment the Sunday before Labor Day. "It's those same pheromones that attract us to them as well. Just think of the virus as a kind of extra-intuitive cruiser on the hunt for the hottest trick."

Doyle worked as a hospital administrator at St. Vincent's which led everyone to believe that his thoughts on medicine and disease were above inquiry from gay hoi polloi like me, a salesman at a used record shop on Jane Street.

"But how are you supposed to protect yourself from getting it?" asked Logan, who had been Kurt's roommate.

"Right now, you should stick with fucking 5s and 6s. Lower if you can find them," Doyle replied.

"I think we all know where we can find those," said another guy, someone who I didn't know. He was wearing jean cut-offs and a tight t-shirt with a banana on it. He was gorgeous.

"Until you hear otherwise, don't stick your dick in anyone remotely attractive," said Doyle. I could feel the guy in the banana shirt looking me up and down.

In the early fall of 1981, the medical establishment informally began calling the disease Hot Guy Flu or, HGF. And just like that, I had my second copyright.

I went to see a matinee of *Only When I Laugh* at the Orpheum on a Wednesday. It had been billed as a comedy in all the previews I'd seen beforehand, however I walked out of the film feeling unusually depressed. Marsha Mason had played the same neurotic actress character she had portrayed in *The Goodbye Girl*, but this time she was also a drunk. Joan Hackett, who played her friend Toby, reminded me too much of the stale older women for whom I'd walk dogs occasionally for extra pocket money. So obsessed with the loss of their beauty that they'd transformed themselves into these bejeweled zombies shut up in their Park Avenue pieds–à–terre, removed from any concept of the real world outside. And, my God, James Coco was just so desperately gay, playing Marsha's most trusted homosexual friend, that you just wanted to shoot him right in the anus. I had gone into the theater for a little afternoon pick-me-up and walked out desperately wanting to have a drink and possibly hang myself.

As I walked down the street thinking more about the film, I spied Anthony, an acquaintance of mine, coming toward me from a half a block away. As soon as he spotted me, he put the back of his hand up to his mouth and affected the most consumptive cough I think I have ever seen outside of a theatrical performance. He looked like he was auditioning for the lead role in *Camille*.

Anthony was very, very average-looking. Not ugly but certainly not anywhere approaching attractive. He was normal looking to a fault. He had a kind of dull, boring look. Nice skin which he clearly moisturized. But he had this very oddly proportioned face. His eyes, for example, were much too far apart, appearing almost alien-like. He had a rather unfortunate nose that most resembled an ancient rocky precipice that had recently lost some of its rocks in an earthquake. No one dreamed about Anthony at night. No one projected Anthony into their nocturnal fantasies or even had him as a distant understudy in their spank bank.

Needless to say, it was with some very firm trepidation that I even ventured to say hello to him as we passed each other. For, without a doubt, saying hello to him would be opening myself up to acknowledge the fact that he was coughing (again, dramatically) at a time when the only gay men coughing on New York City streets were guys with Hot Guy Flu. Anthony was the first instance I had encountered of a mystifying new trend: pretending to have HGF.

It seemed ridiculous. Why would anyone *pretend* to have a deadly disease, especially one that you could get through sex (thereby rendering yourself virtually un-fuckable)? I had to admire him for the boldness of his tactic. But Anthony was really just one in a long line of a history of outcasts mimicking what the popular people are doing.

"How are you, Anthony?" I asked when we locked eyes. He looked around in a world-weary way as if he wasn't quite sure it was him I'd been addressing.

"I haven't been feeling very well. Then I woke up this morning and discovered this." He indicated a purplish mark on his left forearm. It was a new symptom of the disease that hadn't yet been circulated in the newspapers. Doyle had told me about it the week before. I could see that the mark on Anthony's arm had been partly smudged off, perhaps by a passerby on the subway.

"You really should take care of yourself, Anthony." We parted in a foggy, disjointed way and I continued walking down Second Avenue. When I looked back, Anthony was doing his anemic shuffle down the street, looking even more wan, it seemed, from behind.

When I walked into J's Hangout one night in February 1982, there was a guy there who looked exactly like Steven Carrington on *Dynasty*. He had blond wavy hair, a preppy tan cashmere sweater, green eyes that could either look intense or warm depending on the angle with which he directed them toward you. There was something clean and ambrosial about him, like he was a department store mannequin that, usually stationed next to the fragrance counter, had been animated for the night, set free to roam the city. He was leaning up against the bar chatting with the bartender, an older man who'd been working there for years. The bartender kept drying the same glass, so clearly enthralled with Steven Carrington. He had never smiled at me once in all the years I'd been coming there. Not a single time.

I walked past the two of them and made my way to the end of the L-shaped bar so that I might be more visible to Steven Carrington. I took out a cigarette and acted like I was looking around for a light. The bartender, of course, couldn't be bothered to offer me one even though I could see his own cigarette behind the bar sitting in a large glass ashtray with several scrunched up butts. But Steven Carrington immediately saw what I needed and excused himself to go over and offer me a light.

"Thank you," I said to him.

"You're welcome," he replied, smiling which made his eyes open up wider than the real Steven Carrington's ever had on *Dynasty*. The bartender moved to the corner of the bar to wait on another customer.

Hot Guy Flu had suddenly made impossible scenes like this possible. The average looking, the homely, and the downright ugly: all now sexually desirable. Non-carriers of the disease. It had rejected us and now we, the rejected, were the chosen ones.

"I've never seen you at this bar before tonight," he said, putting away his yellow Bic lighter.

"That's funny since I've been coming here for over five years," I answered, perhaps too hastily and with too quick of an attitude.

"I'm sorry. I probably sound like a dick." He brushed his hair back, and rolled his hand down the back of his head to his collar. I suddenly got the sense that he was maniacally horny in that way all men can get.

"It's okay. You just might never have seen me here before," I said.

But he had seen me at J's Hangout before. I know because I hit on him back in '78. He had just put Brainstorm on the jukebox, "Lovin' Is Really My Game." It's a song that has always turned my entire body on. It used to make me feel like I had just been dipped in liquid fire. I would dance to it at Studio 54. Dance and dance and dance. All night. The sweat pouring down my back and pooling in the creases of skin around my body, settling in gulleys around the cushion of back fat that had started developing once I'd hit my late twenties. Just hearing that song that night, I'd felt emboldened enough to hit on

Steven Carrington who'd had his left elbow resting on the jukebox and his pert ass sticking out in faded Levi's for all the bar to see. When I asked him how he was doing, he looked at me like I was a busboy or a barback. I have a "service industry look" one particularly cruel date once told me. Steven Carrington looked at me that night like I was in his way.

Now he looked at me like I was the only man in the room.

"Hey, let's get out of here. I live around the corner."

He had his shirt halfway unbuttoned before he'd even closed the door behind us with his foot. His studio apartment was small and dark, but very clean. A small lamp on a stand near the bed revealed the shadows of a hi-tech style.

Steven Carrington propped himself up on the bed with his Levi's pushed almost down around his thighs. The outline of his dick was pressing hard against his white underwear, struggling to be free. It looked beautiful to me. I held back though. I stood at the foot of his bed to watch him. He still seemed to me like a painting that I was only allowed to look at but never touch for fear that museum security would pull me away and throw me out into the street. That's what the disease had done for us. All those beautiful men in the paintings had been temporarily set free from the confines of their gilded frames, to frolic amidst us mortal folk for a brief time in the cold museum corridors. Gloriously naked, three-dimensional, cut and uncut. Gods hopping off of clouds and landing right in front of us on bewinged feet. We could finally touch them with our human fingers, caress them with our flawed hands. I pulled my t-shirt over my head and slipped out of my own jeans as I walked over to the side of his bed. As I got closer, I could see that Steven's excitement had left a wet spot of precum that was spreading like blood from a puncture wound. I wondered just how long it had been since he'd had sex with another man.

His eyes were closed. I peeled back the elastic lip of his Savile Row briefs and put him in my mouth all the way to the base of his shaft. He let out a groan that seemed to shake his entire body. He grabbed onto the back of my head, right at the base of my skull, and guided my mouth up and down on his cock. I looked up to make eye contact with him, but he was looking up at the ceiling, squinting a bit as if he just might be able to see the small cracks in the imaginary fresco painted above.

Back at The Pines in the summer of 1982, one year after the first cases had begun cropping up, there was a noticeable dearth of good-looking men. Of course, many of them had died during the previous year. But just as many had gone into hiding. Matthew Tone, an ex-model for Halston, had been holed up in his studio apartment for—according to word on the street—two months. Desperate to isolate himself from the disease, he'd created a kind of sealed environment where no one else could touch him. A gay boy in a bubble. Ray Fournier, a dancer for the American School of Ballet and truly one of the most stunning men I'd ever seen, had intentionally cut up his face to make himself appear ugly in order to evade Hot Guy Flu somehow. He'd also stayed inside the entire summer, wrapped in bandages like a mummy, missing rehearsals and auditions, parties and affairs.

Just walking into The Saint, on my first summer Saturday, I couldn't believe what I was seeing. There were maybe four gorgeous alpha men in the entire bar surrounded by gaggles of average-looking guys who looked like me. They would follow each one of the beautiful men around the bar like a pack of rats, chipping and gnawing at the heels of the fellow rat in front of him. Then, when one of the beautiful men had finally decided to give himself over to one of the rats (almost performing a kind of trust fall into the crowd, to be carried away and devoured in a more discrete location) the others would quickly disperse, crawling back into their small holes to await the promise of another tasty morsel that might flutter into their line of sight.

The Hot Guy Flu theory ended abruptly Labor Day weekend. Louis Carney, a morbidly obese felching queen who was infamously known as one of the most unattractive men in New York City (he'd even said it himself) came down with it. Very quickly. One minute he was holding court in a series of video booths at Expressions on 53rd Street and then he was literally on his deathbed at St.

Vincent's (Doyle phoned us all immediately with the news). Like a beached whale, he lay there, in hot pink pajama pants and peroxided hair, his blubber tuffeted around him like a picnic blanket in Central Park. If Louis had it, the disease was not discriminating against anyone. And it could no longer be called HGF. The media had begun referring to it as AIDS. Three letters swapped for four. There was nothing hot about AIDS. Anyone could acquire those letters now.

In January 1983, I found out that Anthony had it—for real this time. Anthony had AIDS. I hadn't really thought about Anthony since I'd run into him that day outside of the movie theater the year before. Actually, I hadn't really thought about the movie I had seen that day either, *Only When I Laugh*. I did hear that James Coco was nominated for an Oscar *and* a Razzie for his performance in it which really just goes to show that a person can look at somebody and see a completely different thing from what another person sees. This is something that has always been the case. Anthony left his group of friends at Danceteria on a Friday night and was dead by Monday morning having expired alone in an emergency room at Beth Israel.

When I heard the news about Anthony, I pictured him in a large, white canopy bed, just like Camille in the play. In my mind, he was wearing a champagne colored robe and staring out the window as if he was watching closely for the cabriolet that would pick him up and take him away.

Sequins at Midnight

Sylvester is mighty real. Mighty real is more than just plain real. It's the kind of real you feel like a punch in the small of your back, a hot rush of amyl nitrate while some man is bearing down on you after a night at The Endup, a dewy kiss on your cheek from your mother. Sylvester sings dark, rich, raw, and mighty real. And it is beautiful.

He sings in the tempo of the times. His voice is like slow, viscous, dark amber honey dripping down a silver, diamond-studded microphone stand. (Goddamn, that should be his next album cover!) There are specks of glitter in the honey from when he shakes his hair. It falls out onto the stage and the audience like it's disco dandruff. Sit down, children, because this is going to be some Josephine Baker shit right up here. A zaftig Josephine Baker. Just as much glamour as the real one (whom Sylvester adores) and all of her stage presence.

Bow down. Nobody gets a show for free. You must pay with your adoration. When you go home and fuck later tonight, you better fuck with the rhythm that I gave you and nobody else's. Because all that rhythm and tempo took years of boiling, decades of churn, centuries of stirring, until it simmers on stage for you tonight for one night only. There are no refunds at the door. Remove your barrettes, unbutton the top button of your shorts, show some belly, lose yourself in the tempered wail of a signature Sylvester falsetto.

Sylvester is on stage beneath the hot colored lights at the Castro Theatre in San Francisco. He looks out into the audience while he is in between "Too Late to Turn Back Now" and his cover of Billie Holiday's "Moonglow" for which he has made a quick costume change. He is performing a "One Night Only" concert tonight. It has been billed as a ten-year retrospective, even though he started performing long before 1974. He thought it sounded better to make it a clean decade. He thought no one would call him out on that. But then, Martha Wash, one of the Tons who's singing backup for him tonight, rolled her eyes as they walked by a poster for the show and said, "Ten years, my fat, black ass!"

He spies Jason and his friends to whom he's given over the entire third row for the midnight show. They're waving at him like hysterical queens. One of them is wearing a tight t-shirt with a Cabbage Patch Doll on it. Sylvester has a black Cabbage Patch Doll at home that he named Nina after Nina Simone. Nina is dressed in a fuchsia-sequined caftan and black rhinestone-studded capri pants that he sewed himself.

Jason's friends are all garish twinks and he loves them, just like he loves Jason. He and Jason had to break up in 1982 because they couldn't move past the fact that they were both total tops. It's such a specifically gay, mechanical problem. Men have been mistaking him for a bottom for years. The Discotays back in Watts thought he was a bottom when he first started hanging out with them because he could turn out such feminine looks, but he wasn't one and he still isn't. He had only ever bottomed at church.

Jason begged him to play "Here Is My Love" from an album of his called *Too Hot to Sleep* that no one bought and he'd all but forgotten about. He wanted Sylvester to play the song just for him.

"That song is a total dud and it's in my man-voice which nobody likes. No, honey. Uh-uh. Not happening," he said as they sat in the middle of his bed one day sorting glass beads, sequins, and cheap little plastic jewels Sylvester uses to make costume jewelry.

"What if I give you something you've always wanted?" Jason said.

And that's when Jason promised he'd give up his ass for Sylvester if he played it tonight. He would bottom for Sylvester. What a bargain! Sylvester has wanted that tight little white ass for as long as he can remember. So it might just be worth it. The band doesn't know he's even considering the song, but they will follow his lead if he wants to play it. The Tons will too. They always do.

He begins to sing "Moonglow" and feels like Billie Holiday would have approved of his rendition. He's wearing a royal blue velour gown with a white crystal headdress, beads hanging down his forehead, and sideburns like a chandelier. When he performs a Billie song, he likes to really put himself in the full Billie mood. Hell, he would shoot up some smack if he thought that would help the song, but he doesn't do needles. Billie wouldn't sing a sad song if she was feeling happy and vice versa. That would've been bullshit and you know people can tell. She would sing a sad song because her heart needed it and she knew the audience needed it as well. That's why she always sounded so damn good. He could always feel every note of what she was singing about. Sylvester is jealous of that. He has sung "Dance (Disco Heat)" before when he didn't feel like it. But the audience didn't know the difference. Only he knew. A small fraud, but one he's rarely pulled over on them.

Sylvester likes to warm up backstage with a bump and a prayer. Martha used to eat a bucket of fried chicken and an orange Nehi before going on, but Sylvester needs a different kind of jolt than just food can provide. Because this is his church. This is gospel, baby. Performing for a crowd is like doing the same thing at church, like when he was a little boy, a wee gayling. The church folks from back in Los Angeles love him now but they didn't always. He started out as their darling little fem boy with beautiful skin and a high, majestic voice like a dazzling chorine, an angel. A little girly, but there are all kinds of queens in church just hiding in plain sight. Nobody cares. Until they do. He had to tell his mother that his anus was ripped up and he needed medical attention. There was no way around it. He was shitting blood. The choir leader, a man in his early forties, had been fucking him. Can you imagine little Sylvester at eleven years old, ankles raised to Jesus or bent over a brocaded chair in the choir room? That's how he first got turned out. But he quite liked it and never considered himself to have been "abused." No, it would have been unfair to use that word. Unfair to those who really had been abused. He never let people say that about him. But when word began to travel around the church about what had happened, it was clear that he was no longer welcome there. No more of his voice of an angel act. He was a fallen angel. Maybe he should have called himself Gabriel on stage later instead of Sylvester. Chocolate Gabriel from the Heavens. Tie him up in black licorice whips and perch him on a cotton candy cloud. That was the last time he ever bottomed.

Bette Midler is in the audience tonight because Sylvester invited her. He was in a movie with her five years ago called *The Rose*. Bette had heard his records and invited him to appear in a scene with her. He played a Diana Ross drag queen. A heftier Diana Ross—Diana Ross after a buffet. Bette's character was supposed to be a Janis Joplinesque singer who comes back to a drag bar she used to patronize. Sylvester was surrounded by a Barbra Streisand queen, a queen dressed as Baby Jane as played by Bette Davis in *What Ever Happened to Baby Jane?*, a Mae West queen, and one that looked like Bette's character in *The Rose*. During filming, he became convinced that the audience would know exactly who all the other white drag queens were but they would think he was just Moms Mabley dressed up in Halston. In the movie, he looks like he's going to step on all of them in order to get onto the stage first (and he would have).

He remembers encountering Bette for the first time years before at the Continental Baths in the Ansonia Hotel when he was in New York performing with the Cockettes. It only cost seven dollars to get inside. A bargain for a man who had always let cash slip through his fingers. He bought two tickets and gave one away to a roadie because nobody else wanted it. Bette sang "Am I Blue?" poolside as a boy did an elegant dive off the board. During her performance, men tried to hand her poppers, but she admitted to the audience that they were hard for straight people to get into. "No one understands what they are," she told them. "What is there to get into?" he remembers wondering. "Just sniff it!" She was so wonderful there in her element. No futz or frills. Just Barry Manilow on the piano, Melissa Manchester as a

Harlette, and Bette singing to the men in towels.

Bette smiles at him from her box seat and he dips himself low to bow to her as he has reached the end of the song. Bette's red hair reads so electric in this light. She reminds him of a madam in a 1920s gay brothel in Chicago which is one of the scenes in his imagination that he keeps alive, adding details here and there whenever he can. He even purchases props for them as if one day he might make the scene come alive. Maybe he will in a music video one day. There she is, Bette-as-madam keeping all the boys in line, paying off policemen who double as customers, turning down the lights in the parlor so the young men she oversees might appear younger against the dusty yellow light under a February moon when they position themselves, languidly draping over upholstered chairs and a fainting couch for the johns who've come to rent them for the night. Maybe he'll tell Bette about this one day. She can help him bring it to life.

There is a short intermission and Sylvester moves backstage to his dressing room. He passes by black balloons and white flowers that are arranged on the stage and make him think he's at a funeral for a mime. He is thinking about the songs left on his playlist. He misses his friend Patrick who would have been here tonight if it wasn't for the simple fact that he is dead now. Dead like so many of the other boys in San Francisco. He can feel it when he walks down the streets now. Men are still partying and cruising each other, sure, but there are somehow not as many as there once were. Or they do it all in secret now somewhere Sylvester has not yet been invited to. Patrick wrote a couple of Sylvester's best songs like "Make it Come Hard" and "Menergy." He helped him create his own publishing company to trademark the songs. It's called Sequins at Noon.

When he comes back out, the stage has darkened and the Tons are singing their slow version of "You Make Me Feel (Mighty Real)" swaying back and forth like a wave is just beneath them. He's supposed to be the match that strikes the beat and brings that song to the real, like they've done before in London, New York, even Huntsville, Alabama once. But there's Jason in the third row looking right up at him with a big smile on his face and it's well after midnight. And he still hasn't played that song for him.

Jackie and Jerry
and The Anvil

Little Edie Beale had opinions about Jackie that she'd never been afraid to share with Jerry.

"Jackie would never have become First Lady if it hadn't been for me. I'm sorry, but that *is* a fact, Jerry. I lost out on getting a Kennedy myself and then Jackie went and married his brother. Everyone knows it, including her. I'm not jealous or anything for saying that out loud," she said while setting out slices of bread for the raccoons that lived in her attic.

"Isn't she your cousin though?" Jerry asked.

"Yes, she's my cousin. Cousin Jacqueline. So? God!"

Little Edie paused to glance out the window, seemingly caught up in a brief moment from the past that was taking place just beyond the overgrown Spanish wall garden that began beneath the back porch and then extended out to the sliver of ocean that was visible to them from the second floor. This was something Jerry often saw her do. "Jackie's more *jolie-laide* than I am, if you know what I mean. I used to be a very great beauty. The most beautiful debutante of East Hampton. They called me 'Body Beautiful Beale,' I am sure you have heard." Jerry had heard—from Little Edie herself and on several occasions. "Here, I can find the news clippings if you give me a minute."

Wearing a magenta and brown paisley bathing suit with a turquoise wall hanging wrapped around her head festooned with a chipped scarab brooch, Little Edie began rummaging through a stack of yellowing newspapers. Jerry spied a centipede the size of a Kit Kat slowly creeping its way across the front page of *The Hampton Gazette*. She didn't see it so he simply let it pass as he often did with things he saw—live things—while he was visiting Little Edie and her mother, Big Edie, at Grey Gardens. "Jackie is sweet and all but she's always been quite breathy. Honestly, you can't hear a word she's saying half the time."

"She seemed real nice when I saw her on TV," said Jerry.

"Yes, well, she does come off that way," Little Edie said. She carefully moved aside a dark navy blue blanket with a white anchor stitched on it. Ari Onassis had given it to her and Big Edie shortly before he died, and they now referred to it exclusively as "The Onassis Blanket." "Don't get me wrong, Jerry. I think Jackie's darling."

Jerry first met Jackie on a fall afternoon a couple

days later. He'd been painting the front porch railing of Grey Gardens when a big black town car pulled right up to the house. At first, he thought it might be another fan who had seen the documentary and had now come to gawk at the Beales or attempt to gain an autograph (which both of the women honestly loved to give out). If Jerry was around when that sort of thing happened, he'd usually only let them get as close as the fence to snap a few pictures but not any closer. One time, a couple of them had tried to enter the kitchen through a back window that had a broken latch and he'd had to run them off the property. He'd also chased away some teenagers trying to saw off bits and pieces of the house as mementos. A fan once left a basket of food for the two women, but Little Edie thought it might be poisoned so she brought it in the house and let the raccoons have at it. She kept a cap gun upstairs to scare off intruders but, as of yet, he had never seen her use it.

While he was still sizing up the town car, a driver exited from the front to open the rear-side passenger door. A woman stepped out wearing a pale yellow kerchief over her hair and a large pair of sunglasses. He put down his paintbrush and walked toward the car.

He was wearing a dirty gray *Newsday* sweatshirt that day, which happened to be the same sweatshirt that he had worn in one of the scenes that had made it into the documentary. Albert and David Maysles, the directors, had scoffed at him during filming when he suggested running out to his car to get a fresh shirt the day they filmed him. "Authentic," they called him. Just like Little Edie had said about him when he had first showed up at the front door of the mansion for the first time to see if anyone lived there. Little Edie had opened the door, much to his surprise, and exclaimed, "Oh, my God—the Marble Faun has arrived."

He hadn't heard of *The Marble Faun* at the time. Later when he looked it up, he discovered that it was a reference to a very famous work by Nathaniel Hawthorne. *The Marble Faun* was a classic male beauty of Greek antiquity. He had been very flattered by what he took as a complimentary comparison. It was only later that he learned that the statue upon which the book had been titled possessed pointy ears. Were his ears what Little Edie had first noticed about him? "You do have a beautiful face, Jerry, just like a girl. You look like my mother. The absolute image of my mother," Little Edie had said to him in the movie.

He watched the woman step out of the car. And then he froze in place: a satyr at rest, chiseled in marble, pointy ears alert.

Just a few yards in front of him stood the Former First Lady of the United States and, miraculously, she was extending her hand to him.

"My Aunt Edith and my cousin have both grown quite fond of you. They trust you."

"Yes, thank you, ma'am. I'm here to help with anything possible."

"Please, call me Jackie." She had a very kind way about her. Dignified, yet accessible. Jerry suddenly became self-conscious that he was wearing only the sweatshirt.

"I'm Jerry."

"It's very nice to meet you, Jerry. I'm expecting workmen to arrive tomorrow to continue renovations on the house. I'm trying to get it just a little closer to what it looked like when my sister Lee and I were girls. Would you be willing to let them into the mansion?"

"Yes, of course," Jerry answered. Jackie hadn't needed to say it, but leaving something like that up to the Edies probably wasn't the best idea. Big Edie, for one, rarely, if ever, left her room.

"Excellent! It's settled then," she said.

"Is that Jacqueline out there, Jerry?" yelled Big Edie from an open upstairs window.

"Yes, Aunt Edith, it's me," she answered.

Little Edie poked her head out of the same window. "Don't come in, Jackie! We're not prepared for a guest." Jackie smiled at Jerry. Her gentle smile made him feel like a companion or a friend rather than just the handyman or the help. She instantly made him feel special.

Jackie suggested that they have gimlets together on the front lawn.

Jackie came to the house every couple of weeks to check

on the progress of the construction work and Jerry would often be there to provide her with updates. Little Edie didn't understand why Jerry or Brooks, the Beales's off-and-on gardener, couldn't perform the construction themselves.

"There are perfect strangers just traipsing through our house. God, Mother or I could be raped!" she howled to Jerry.

Jackie had effectively quartered herself to the porch during her visits. Jerry was sure this was due to either the fetid smell of the interior of the house or the fleas that covered Jerry's ankles when he was up in Big Edie's bedroom for a visit or to eat corn on the cob prepared on her bedside Sterno. Jackie was too classy to ever mention the odor of the house or its many pests. There also seemed to be an unspoken agreement between Jackie and Little Edie that she would stay outside during her visits.

"I'd like you to escort me out tonight. You can take me to a club," Jackie said one day as she leaned against the railing while Jerry was smoking on the porch. She reached over and took the cigarette from him for a drag. She was wearing a rust-colored shade of lipstick that left a mark on the cigarette.

"For serious?" Jerry asked. He couldn't imagine bringing Jacqueline Bouvier Kennedy Onassis to any of the bars he frequented. "I'm nobody. Why would you want to go out with me?"

"You're not nobody, Jerry. I've told you how important you are to this house and to my aunt and cousin. And you've become important to me, too. So I won't hear any of that kind of talk." She handed the cigarette back to him and held his gaze firmly. "I'm being perfectly serious. I want you to accompany me. Is there a club you know of in the city? I don't care where we go, just as long as it's somewhere you like."

"Sure, I know someplace we can go."

When they pulled up to The Anvil on West 14th Street later that night in Jackie's town car, Jerry witnessed a long line of guys waiting outside to get in. Most of the men waiting in line were wearing some kind of leather accouterments—assless chaps, harnesses, leather caps, armbands. One man was in a camouflage leather jockstrap. Jerry saw a ballet dancer he knew named Ray Fournier. Ray had his back turned and there was a navy blue handkerchief poking out of the right back pocket of a pair of Levi's that almost looked like they'd been painted onto his muscled legs, each thigh bulging in an entasis.

Jackie laughed and remarked, "This was not exactly what I had in mind."

"I'm sorry. You said to pick somewhere I go and, well, this is where I go. Maybe we should drive around and find someplace else," he suggested.

"No, no. Let's go in. I'm sure it'll be fantastic." Jackie had pulled her hair back tight and she wore a pair of glasses with lenses that had a slight purplish tint to them so he couldn't really tell at any moment whether or not she was looking at him. She began to button her camel-colored cashmere coat. It was by Halston. He could see from the label.

Jerry didn't know why she was sure that it would be fantastic. Or why she was sure of anything. He knew *he'd* be fine, but he honestly couldn't recall ever having seen a woman inside The Anvil. A biological woman, that is. There'd been drag queens there before, but the place was meant for gay men. And it smelled like men. What would happen to a woman there, he did not know. And he didn't think that Jacqueline Bouvier Kennedy Onassis was the ideal test case to find out.

"What if they recognize you?" Jerry asked.

"And if they do?"

William Friedkin, director of *The Exorcist*, had filmed a couple scenes at The Anvil for an Al Pacino movie called *Cruising* in 1979. It was about a cop who goes undercover into the hardcore gay leather scene in order to catch a serial killer. Jerry had been there one night, dancing on the bar in just his jockstrap, so he appeared in the background of a scene as an extra. He got paid $25 and a free tube of lubricant. A production assistant asked him to show up the next night for re-shoots. There were several gays protesting outside of the bar during the second night of filming, but Jerry just strode right past them like he was a movie star or something.

"You Uncle Bottom!"

"Fuck you, you pig!"

"They hate us!"

All that damn racket over a movie. And with Al Pacino too. Hadn't they ever seen *Dog Day Afternoon* or *The Godfather*? It was Pacino for fuck's sake, he's a legend. Jerry never played up his own celebrity, but, to his credit, *Cruising* was actually the second movie in which he'd appeared. He'd only been recognized in public once for being in *Grey Gardens* and it was by an Asian woman who owned the bodega near his apartment. She had been strangely insistent that Big and Little Edie were the same homeless women who had shoplifted from her store in 1967.

"I see them! She take Wonder Bread and batteries!" Mrs. Chan had told him.

"Well, that's impossible. They never leave the house. And they weren't in New York City in the '60s at all ever!"

"Harold, we'll be exiting here. Please swing back around in an hour," Jackie told the driver who was so quiet up front that Jerry had forgotten about him entirely.

"Yes, ma'am," Harold stated as he came around to her side of the car to open the door.

Jerry knew The Anvil's doorman (biblically), so he and Jackie were able to bypass the line and walk right in. Suddenly, he *wanted* someone to recognize her. Maybe he could be famous again by association. Little Edie went into Manhattan for the first time in over a decade when *Grey Gardens* first premiered. He imagined she must have felt as important as he did now. He could never understand why he hadn't received an invitation to that premiere. He was part of the cast of the film. The Maysles really should have invited him too.

When they walked into The Anvil, the familiar smell of the place hit him like a hot wave. It was a strange brew of sweat, poppers, and meat as if the space, which had formally been home to a slaughterhouse at the turn-of-the-century, had retained the tangy aroma of sirloins and linked sausages through the decades, letting hog-stink sweat out of the walls.

"Let's get a drink. What will you have, Jackie?"

"I think I'd like a beer." She was staring at a rather hirsute man sitting against the wall, shirtless and covered in matted chest hair with smaller mustachioed men perched on each knee.

"Coming right up," he said.

Jackie brought her hand up to her forehead in a gesture of retreat. "I feel like Jane Goodall in here," she said.

"Step back and observe the species as we operate in our natural habitat," Jerry said.

The man who Jerry had tried to attract the night he'd been dancing on the bar at The Anvil was the friend of a guy he'd met at the Y, a lawyer named Gregory. Jerry had met Gregory a couple of times in passing without, he thought, making much of an impression. He didn't really know how to talk to a lawyer. But that night (the same night he made it into *Cruising* as an extra) he had stripped down to his jockstrap and climbed on top of the bar still wearing tube socks, not giving a good old shit. He danced up and down the slick bar, bending over to wag his ass in the air. There was a trapeze bar up there from which he swung, dangling in front of the crowd. He caught Gregory looking over a couple times and would turn his back to him each time he made it to the back end of the bar so he could show off what he thought of as his best side—his ass. Gregory had been dressed in a red flannel shirt and had a slightly reddish beard, not something Jerry had seen before. He felt like it was a little surprise since Gregory was actually a blond. He wondered what other surprises Gregory might have to share with him.

"What do you usually do here?" Jackie asked.

"You're kind of looking at it," Jerry answered. He didn't think he should show her how he walked on the bar ... and he wasn't wearing a jockstrap or tube socks.

"If I were you, Jerry, I'd do it all. I'd do everything."

"Funny. You know your cousin Edie would probably say the same thing to me."

"She would," Jackie agreed. "What's downstairs?" She was motioning toward a man who was heading down a back staircase.

"Nothing *you* need to know anything about, that's for sure," he said. "And don't bother with that door marked 'Ladies Room.' It's really just an exit out onto the street."

"Mmm hmm," Jackie said. Although he couldn't see her eyes, he could tell that one of her eyebrows was arched and she was smirking at him. "I'll be the judge of what I need to know, Jerry."

The stairs led to the basement of the club's underground. It was quite a seedy place. There were dark passageways where all the hookup action took place. Jerry remembered looking up through the grates when he ended up down there once searching for the bathroom. The endless corridors felt like tunnels in a French Resistance movie. He once ran into the German avant-garde director Rainer Werner Fassbinder, all clad in leather. He'd seen Fassbinder in his movie *Fox and His Friends* which had come out the same year as *Grey Gardens* and had been playing at the same movie theater in the Village.

A small stage at the back of the bar lit up and a smattering of men moved toward the center of the bar, drinks in hand. They all started directing their attention to a model house that was slowly being lowered onto the stage from the rafters attached to black leather cords. "Paint it Black" by The Rolling Stones began to play. The model was cut just like a dollhouse with the cross-section of the house visible to the audience. In the attic level of the house there was a woman (biological? Jerry couldn't tell yet at this point) whose body was contorted in such a way that she was able to fit inside the small space. She was wearing a white blouse, a dark sweater with a yellow Star of David, a mid calf length dark skirt, and knee socks. She was holding a small red notebook in her left hand. Just as the house had reached a sufficient distance, she slowly began to extricate herself from the attic level of the model.

The woman, who was now very obviously a drag queen, placed her black stiletto heels on the bare wooden stage, her shapely legs, much too reminiscent of a horny, available woman on a Saturday night, were entirely too lithe and muscled to be a young woman's, as her outfit seemed to convey. Syncopated with the music, each leg had come out of the human pretzel in a full extension and then the queen took over the space with a series of gyrating contortions.

"I think that's supposed to be Anne Frank," Jackie said, her mouth hanging open in an expression Jerry had not seen on her before.

"I believe you're right," Jerry said.

Anne Frank produced a lighter from under her wig, her hair pulled back behind her ears and held up with bobby pins. She lit the fireplace of the model and then pulled two long rods from the structure and stuck the tips of each one into the fire. She bent over backwards and lifted one of the rods, now alit with fire, opened up her mouth and stuck the flaming rod down her throat.

Then she did the same with the other. The crowd erupted into elated gasps and applause, some laughter, everyone having abandoned, for the moment, the groping and kissing in which they'd been engaged when Jackie and Jerry had first entered.

Anne Frank turned to the audience with a solemn expression on her face as if she were being made to perform that night against her will. She took one of the rods, now wiped clean of fire, and brought back the flame by sticking the tip into the lit fireplace of the model. She lit the model on fire from below and began to climb back into the attic, each limb somehow folding into itself like retractable walking sticks. The house burned as it was lifted back into the air and then disappeared up into the rafters.

"I used to be a little bit wild. Carefree and wild like you wouldn't believe," Jackie said.

They had left The Anvil and were now back in the car.

"Like, fire-eating-drag-queen-contortionist-wild?"

"Well, nothing that would make anyone blush these days, that's for sure. And certainly not anyone at *that* place. But I was wild in just the kind of way I needed to be at a certain time in my life. I'm sure you can understand something like that. Can't you?" She rested her right hand on his arm.

"Well, sure, I can. I was voted 'Mr. Club Baths 1977' myself. I even beat out a Colt model for the title."

"Look at you!" Jackie touched his arm lightly. "Although I don't know what Colt means, I saw a couple men tonight at that bar who probably voted for you." Jerry smiled and looked down into his lap, unsure where to put his hand, Jackie's still on his arm.

"So what did you do that was so wild?" Jerry asked. They had just passed by a corner in the Village where Jerry's friend had once picked up a man who later tied him up and left him in his apartment for several hours only to come back and fuck him with a blindfold on. He had a feeling that Jackie's version of "wild" might be a bit different from his.

Jackie told Jerry about the time during her teenage years when she'd been living in McLean, Virginia, close to Washington, D.C. "Right across the old Chain Bridge is where my stepfather's estate was." She told him about an older boy and his family who moved into the guesthouse of the estate. "His name was Charles and he was amazingly beautiful. Tall, brown eyes, by far the most handsome boy I'd ever seen. He was three years older than me and I had an enormous crush on him. The first crush I think I ever had."

"Did you do anything about it?" Jerry asked.

"One night I threw a handful of pebbles at his window. Stupid and childish. But he snuck out to meet me just the same. I didn't know what we should do, so I suggested that we take my stepfather's car for a joy ride in Georgetown."

"Ha! Did you?"

"Yes we did. And *I* was the one who drove, much to Charles's chagrin. Oh, how he protested! You really could have hit him over with a feather that night."

"How do you mean?" Jerry asked.

"You see, I had always been a bit shy around him before that night. I didn't really know what to do when you had a crush on a boy and so I didn't do much of anything besides act like a little fool. My sister Lee, who is younger than me, could always just go right up to Charles and talk to him without a second thought. But I normally wouldn't have dared. Oh no. Never."

"What was so different about that night? What made you take a chance?" Jackie took off her glasses. Jerry could see her face soften as she fell further into reverie. Years shed from her face and her eyes had seemed, to him at least, to brighten. All the things she had been through, all the tragedy in her life, before her, not behind her.

"I don't know, actually. The moon was so bright that night; it must have inspired me. It was a perfect night. I drove us around and we got stopped by a patrol car somewhere around MacArthur Boulevard, I think. I talked the officer out of giving us a ticket which I think impressed Charles."

"Whatever happened to him?" Jerry asked her.

"He moved to California and had a wife and five

children. We used to send each other letters. I hadn't heard from him for several years and then I found out he had left his family and moved to Manhattan. He works as a stockbroker now and lives on Horatio Street."

"We just passed Horatio," Jerry said.

"I know," she answered. "A couple months ago, Charles contacted me to ask if I could help him track down a copy of a book called *Island in the Sky* by Ernest K. Gann. It's been out of print for years and he was trying to obtain a copy of it for a client of his. Have you ever read it?"

"Can't say that I have," Jerry answered.

"Out of nowhere, he sent me a formal letter at Viking saying that he had been in every bookstore in town looking for this book and it had finally dawned on him that I might be able to help him locate it. He was looking for me. After all this time. It's funny, isn't it? How people you never thought you'd ever see again can suddenly pop back up into your life. Like ghosts."

"Little Edie said that there's a ghost at Grey Gardens. His name is Cap and he was involved with her in the 1950s.

"You know about Cap?" Jackie asked.

"Yeah. He was married and he was fooling around with her on the side or something? She told me and Lois about him. Lois lived with the Edies about five years ago. Lois even painted a portrait of him for Little Edie that's hanging in one of the upstairs bedrooms."

"I think there's a portrait of him in Washington somewhere. Cap was Secretary of Interior under Truman," said Jackie.

"Wow," said Jerry.

"She talks about him in that movie you're both in, you know. 'The married man.' That's Cap. And would you like to hear the funniest thing? Charles was Cap's son-in-law."

"Your Charles? No way. How?" Jerry asked.

"Well, Charles married Cap's daughter, Marilyn. I actually went to school with her at Holton-Arms, but she was older than me." Jackie threw her head back and looked at the roof of the car and laughed. "And here we are—men from the same family again. I'm sure that's how Edie would put it."

"She would," said Jerry, chuckling. "Her man is a ghost though. Yours is still alive."

"He was never more than just a good friend," she said. "This is my building. Would you like to come up for a drink?"

"I appreciate the offer, ma'am—Jackie. But no thanks. I think I'll say goodnight to you here."

"Thank you for tonight, Jerry. I've had more fun than I think you'll ever know." She put out her hand for Jerry to shake. Without much thought, Jerry took it, brought it up to his lips, and gave her a kiss on the knuckles, bony and pronounced enough for him to slightly finger the small valleys in between each ridge.

"Good night, Jackie."

"Please, use the car. Harold will take you anywhere you need to go. Good night." Jackie exited the car, holding her camel-colored coat close to herself at the neck in a way that reminded Jerry of Little Edie holding onto her fur coat in the movie poster for *Grey Gardens*.

He'd seen the poster in a marquee window at the 8th Street Playhouse when it first came out and he finally got to see it after the premiere. In the poster, Little Edie stands in front of the ruins of the house. It almost looks like an advertisement for a horror film: a strange woman standing outside of a creepy, condemned manse, large brambles and brush overgrown so much on the left-hand side, tree branches have engulfed the house, rending their way into each broken window, through holes dug out by the raccoons, through the spaces in between the floorboards, circumventing Little Edie's mementos hung on the wall, curling their way around Big Edie's bedside Sterno.

The red lipstick that Little Edie wears in the poster is set against her pale, downturned face, complementing a red ribbon that ties her headscarf into place. She must have instinctively known to add a pop of color to draw the focus further toward herself amidst all that gray. As if he could be looking anywhere else. She is wearing a long brown fur coat, which is ragged and missing tufts of fur along its arms. The coat was a gift to her from Cap twenty-five years before the picture was taken.

Her right hand is in the front pocket of the coat, her wrist surrounded by a large, generous sleeve. But the other hand is pulling one side of the coat across her, protectively it seemed to Jerry, as if she is holding onto the privilege of love the coat once afforded her. Holding onto the past.

"Where to, sir?" Harold asked him from the front seat.

"Back to The Anvil," Jerry said.

At Danceteria

Ten people must have immediately looked at Keith when he walked through the door. He saw a couple of them do that thing where they quickly whispered something to the person they were talking to ("Oh, my God, do you know who that is?") then left their friend like a bad hookup, zooming over to him, as if on a conveyor belt. Somehow it never got old. In fact he still wasn't used to it; he wanted more.

"Keith, I loved the mural you did last week on that brick wall!"

"Happy Birthday, Keith! There's some blow in the bathroom downstairs. Last stall on the left. All you want, babe. Tell them Nance sent you."

"Have you seen El Cid? He's looking for you. A warning, though—he's been doing lines all afternoon. He's horny as fuck, but probably can't, you know, do anything."

Keith was happily surprised by the turnout for his

birthday. He adjusted his glasses. They had gotten a bit grimy from sweat and city detritus earlier that day when he had painted an abandoned school bus in Brooklyn. Flecks of yellow and blue paint dotted the corners of each lens and appeared to him like the *Bang! Pow! Bam! Zoink!* stars from the *Batman* episodes of his youth.

"Give me a fucking drink!" he shouted above the music to no one in particular. His vibe was nerdy-cool but with substance. New Wave Aspirational. Tonight he was doing Horny Fucked-Up Celebrity Turns Twenty-Six.

Madonna took to the stage and started singing "Dress You Up." She was wearing an orange jacket and skirt covered in a print from one of Keith's paintings.

"God. Fuck. There you are, finally," Kenny said, handing him a beer.

"Someone's already getting me a drink."

"So you'll have two then. What's the problem? Besides, you'll need them both once I tell you what happened last night."

"You finally got laid?" Keith asked.

"Michael died."

"Michael. Michael Strover? Fuck me. I didn't even know he was sick."

"A week ago he wasn't," Kenny said. "Remember when we used to call him *Ms.*? Like the magazine?"

Keith took a swig from his beer and set it down on a nearby table. Then someone handed him a SoCo and lime, with an incongruous lemon wedge on the side. "This never would have happened if I were still working here," he said, gesturing toward the errant lemon.

"Keith, I slept with Michael Strover last Christmas."

He looked at Kenny and ran his free hand over his rapidly receding hairline as he peered off toward the stage. "I can't do the babies anymore ... and the guy juggling the smaller little guys and the kids holding hands across the globe, except they're also holding on so they won't fall off. It's got to be more now, you know? More 1984. Something is fucking happening here."

Madonna kept singing on the stage.

Keith had heard that song of hers three years earlier on her demo tape. It had been a much scratchier recording, and she had played it for him on her boom box during one of their smoke breaks. He'd been a busboy at the West 37th Street location when Madonna had worked as a coat check girl. They'd point out the cute butts on the waiters while they smoked Pall Malls. Madonna was always so loud and sure of herself, which Keith liked because he always thought he was going to be something big too.

"I'm gonna call you the Virgin Mary. Or VM for short. That'll be my nickname for you. Or Mo. Do you like Mo?" Keith had told her.

"VM? Are you mad? That makes me sound like some kind of vaginal plague. 'This one has VM, Doc. Do you have your gas mask on?' No, Keith. It's Madonna. It's always been Madonna, and it'll always be Madonna. Just Madonna. Like Cleopatra. Or Cher."

"Madonna. Got it."

She had kissed him on the cheek and hopped off to her post at the coat check.

Keith looked out over the crowd of people dancing furiously to her song. The strobe lights from the balcony flickered in just the right way so that, for a second, everyone looked as if they were frozen in time, suspended from the ceiling by wires. Not only suspended in place, though, but also enveloped by the person next to them, sucked into them. Then everything would black out. And there'd be another frozen tableau, ever changing. It would arise for a glimmer of an instant to take the place of the last. Nothing stayed the same. Ever.

He noticed a ladder leaning against a large white column. It must've been left over from an electrician working on Danceteria's vast lighting system. He ditched his drink and headed to it, climbed right up to the top step—always nimble. He could remain steady on almost any surface. He pulled out one of the thick black Sharpies he always kept in his back pocket and began to draw on the white column that prevented the roof from caving in on them. He drew a man with a hole in his stomach, a hole big enough for the head of another man to peak his head through. And then that man's arm was shoved into the pubic area of another one. The one with the arm up his pubic area had both of his feet in the mouths of two other little men. Small double parentheses came off at points of pressure, like overexaggerated sweat—a thrust here, a creaky withdrawal there. Near each hole he drew tiny little men falling out like byproducts of energy spent, expectorant.

Madonna started singing "Where's the Party?" and gestured toward Keith with her microphone for the refrain. With each step he came farther down the ladder and the column, connecting the little men he drew in a never-ending tapestry of penetration.

"Ladies and gentlemen, Mr. Keith Haring! Happy Birthday, Keith!" she yelled into the microphone. He grabbed a tube of lipstick from a girl wearing a black Bronski Beat shirt hanging off her left shoulder. Scrambling back up the ladder, he colored in the crevices between the bodies, the splash points of entry. Fire-engine red. Anal reds bleeding into the column. They were New Wave hieroglyphics. The story of our times.

Acknowledgments

I have many people to thank for helping me bring this collection, and the characters in its pages, to life (and, in the case of this book, *back* to life). They all contributed to the book in various ways that proved invaluable to me. Listed in no particular order, they are: Emily Voorhees, Megan Byrne, Anne Marie Morris, Julie Morris, Jonathan Church, Daniel Robert Weinberg, Diana Metzger, Diesel Robertson, K. Tyler Christenson, Sharan Z Jayne, Mafalda Marrocco, Tom Doolittle, Alice I. Lee, Kathleen Rawson, Patrick Geary, William Geary, James Owen Dunn III, George Young Warner, Carla Nassy, Nicholas Galbraith, Steven Siegel, Mona Z. Kraculdy, Elise Levine, Stephanie Grant, Richard McCann, Andrew Holleran, Amanda Powell Walker, and members of the Sophistigay Book Club of Washington, D.C.

In the course of my research, I found several books immensely helpful. These books include: *Simply Halston* by Steven Gaines, *Halston: An American Original* by Elaine Gross and Fred Rottman, *Rock Hudson: His Story* by Rock Hudson and Sara Davidson, *My Life at Grey Gardens: 13 Months and Beyond* by Lois Wright and Andrew Afram, and *The Fabulous Sylvester: The Legend, The Music, The Seventies in San Francisco* by Joshua Gamson.

Special thanks to Raymond Luczak for first publishing several of these stories in *Jonathan: A Queer Fiction Journal* and encouraging me to use them as the starting point for a full collection. I'd also like to acknowledge his brilliant editing and his role as the tireless midwife of this book.

I must also express my gratitude to my loving parents, Grover and Maggi Walker, for always encouraging me to create goals in life and then work hard to make them happen.

—PDW

About the Author

Philip Dean Walker is a Pushcart Prize nominee whose work has appeared in literary journals such as *Big Lucks, Collective Fallout, Jonathan, Glitterwolf Magazine, theNewerYork, Driftwood Press, Lunch Review,* and *Carbon Culture Review.* His short story "Three-Sink Sink" was named as a finalist for the 2013 Gertrude Stein Award in Fiction from *The Doctor T.J. Eckleburg Review* and appears in the anthology *Pay for Play* (Bold Strokes Books). He holds a B.A. in American Literature from Middlebury College and an M.F.A. in Creative Writing (Fiction) from American University. He lives in Washington, D.C. This is his first book.

philipdeanwalker.com

CPSIA information can be obtained
at www.ICGtesting.com
Printed in the USA
LVOW12s1626160517
534727LV00001B/86/P